Lum

Lum

a novel

Libby Ware

SHE WRITES PRESS

Published 2015
Printed in the United States of America
ISBN: 978-1-63152-003-7
Library of Congress Control Number: 2015937596

For information, address:
She Writes Press
1563 Solano Ave #546
Berkeley, CA 94707

She Writes Press is a division of SparkPoint Studio, LLC.

This is a work of fiction. Names, characters, places, and incidents either are the product of the author's imagination or are used fictitiously. Any resemblance to actual persons, living or dead, is entirely coincidental.

Chapters 1–3 of this book were originally published in slightly different form as a short story, "The Circuit," in *Feminist Studies*, Fall 2009, Volume 35, #3.

To my mother, for the stories
and for sharing her love of reading

The Little Room
Off the Porch

1933

L um leaned forward in the passenger seat as if to help the black
1930 Ford pickup struggle up the muddy road. Her brother Jimmy
floored the accelerator.

"You should get Al to look at the truck. He's real good with engines,"
Lum offered.

Jimmy snorted. "She just don't like hills."

The right front tire sank into a huge hole, lurching Lum against the
dash. Jimmy downshifted. "Just sit back, Lum, this road is awful. Al
ought to fix these holes."

Lum eased back, wide thighs spreading under her faded black corduroy dress. Gullies full from heavy rains lined High Ford Road. On
a good day it was hard for two cars to pass each other, but now the
truck rode right in the middle. Cows grazed behind barbed wire fence,
stepping through rivulets in search of grassy tufts. Lum was relieved
when she saw the familiar clapboard farmhouse. They stopped by the
weathered porch.

"Well, here you go, Lum." Jimmy stomped on the brake, opened the
door with the engine still coughing, and heaved a leather valise out
of the truck bed. "What the hell you got in this thing? Your favorite
rocks?" He snickered as he carried it up the granite steps. Lum lifted a
carpetbag, the fabric's color and pattern obscured by age. It was because
of Jimmy and her other brothers that she was called "Lum." She was

1

named Columbia, but her brothers couldn't pronounce it, so she was nicknamed Lum. When she was in high school, she tried to get people to call her Columbia, but her childhood name stuck.

"Hey, Lum." A skinny, red-haired woman came out to the porch, a squirming baby on her hip.

"Hey, Jimmy," she added, brushing a damp curl off her forehead.

Jimmy grunted, set down the valise, and trudged back to his truck.

"Cousin Margaret, how are you?" Lum said as she put down the carpetbag.

"My rheumatism's acting up. This weather don't do it no good." Margaret shifted the baby to the other hip. "Baby Meg's about to drive me mad, teething and all. I'm glad to see you. You're so good with the children."

"I learned on you, dear. You were such a good baby." Lum held out her broad hands. "My sweet Meg, come here. You remember Auntie Lum, don't you?" The baby drew back, hiding her face in her mother's bosom.

Jimmy stood with one foot in the shuddering truck. "I'm gonna get on now, Lum. You'll be back next winter, huh?"

"I reckon, Jimmy." Relieved to be leaving Jimmy and Ethel's, but wary about being with Al and Margaret, Lum hoped this visit wouldn't end like the last one. She picked up her bags, the valise pulling her off balance, and headed toward the front door.

"Lum, Al and me," Margaret said haltingly, "we thought, well, you could stay in this little room off the porch." Margaret stared past Lum's shoulder. "Since Caleb's getting so big and all, it ain't right to share his room. You understand, don't you?"

Lum turned abruptly into the small enclosure on the porch so Margaret wouldn't see her blush. In all her thirty-three years, she'd never been relegated to an outside place. The room had been built for circuit preachers or judges, but lately, ever since the bad times brought on by Hoover, was used by men who worked a day or two for Al. Lum put the carpetbag on the narrow bed and lugged the leather case to the corner. A wisteria vine invaded the room through a broken windowpane.

Margaret stood at the threshold, the baby whimpering and twisting in her arms. "She cried for weeks after you left last fall. Maybe you can calm her down." She passed Meg to Lum.

Lum touched the baby's chin. "What's a matter with my Meg?" Lum bounced her up and down until the baby giggled. "You're the best little girl in the Shenandoah Valley, maybe all of Virginia, yes you are."

"Lum, you get settled in. I gotta get back to the kitchen. Al and Kenny will be in for lunch before you know it. You don't mind keeping an eye on Meg, do you?"

"That's why I'm here." She jostled the baby up and down playfully. "Meg, be a good girl and stay still while I unpack." Laying Meg on the center of the wedding ring quilt, Lum noticed several patches were missing or worn thin. She remembered helping her grandmother sew the quilt when Cousin June was pregnant with Margaret. Lum knew then that she would never get a wedding quilt or any of the other things that went with being a bride.

Whining, the baby kicked and thrashed her balled fists. "What's all this fidgeting about, Meg? You teething? We'll get you fixed up soon." Lum opened her carpetbag, took out two cotton dresses, smoothed the fabric, and laid them in the bottom drawer of the unpainted pine dresser. White underclothes and black wool stockings went in another drawer. Next she laid a straight-edge razor and some soap powder on the dresser top. Last, Lum unpacked a gingham apron. After she slipped it over her shoulders and tied it around her waist, she picked up Meg. "Let's go see what your mama's doing."

Margaret was at the kitchen table with a nubby summer squash in one hand and a paring knife in the other. "So, how are Jimmy and Ethel doing? Still at each other's throats?" Margaret sliced the red-handled knife back and forth in the air.

Lum couldn't help laughing. She tried to stay loyal to each of her kin who gave her a home, however temporary, but she knew more about each of them than she wanted. "I reckon they won't kill each other. They wouldn't have nobody to fight with."

Meg whimpered, so Lum started bouncing her on her knee. "Little girl, little girl, riding into town, take care, little girl, don't you fall down!" Lum spread her legs and Meg fell into the black corduroy hammock, giggling. "Margaret, don't you have some persimmon bark?"

"Think so. Look in the cabinet for the amber bottle. That spring tonic from Doc Meadows tastes like it's mostly persimmon." She twisted her mouth and stuck out her tongue.

"Best thing in the world for teething." Lum mixed the tonic and some honey with her finger and put her thick forefinger into Meg's mouth.

"Lum, you are such a saint. I wish you could cure my rheumatism. I get so I can't do nothing. Al thinks I'm being lazy, but you know that ain't so."

"You know, Margaret, there are as many remedies for rheumatism as there are plants in the woods, but there's only one that works. Sleep. You sleep good and your joints are limber as a cat's. Sleep bad and you're in for a whole lot of pain." Meg sucked Lum's finger.

"What? Sleep with a young'un crying half the night and the bull-frogs making a god-awful racket? Not to mention Al coming in lord knows when."

"Caleb coming home to eat?" Lum asked. Meg's mouth grew slack and Lum cradled the tiny head as the baby's breathing slowed into sleep.

"No, he's helping Miss Shay with the younger ones, so he carries his lunch. Kenny Doyle will be here, though. He's been working with Al since he got out of the pen last fall." Margaret cut a piece of fat off of the ham and put it into the pan of beans. "Wish I could make biscuits good as you, Lum. But I reckon I'll just whip up some corn muffins."

"You want me to make some biscuits, just say so, you don't have to pussyfoot around your old Lum. I was making biscuits before you ever saw the light of day. Not that there's anything wrong with corn muffins. I can eat 'em any day of the week."

Margaret rose and lifted the sleeping child. "I'm gonna lay down with Meg for a bit before Al and Kenny get here for dinner."

Lum grabbed an oak dough bowl and rubbed the hand-carved edge, smooth from eight decades of women's hands. She dug out a handful of flour from a collapsed burlap sack and sprinkled it in the bowl.

Pie-Making

1908

Luuuum, Lum! Come on in, Lum." Lum wanted to continue to the lake, but she turned around to see her grandmother in the doorway holding the dough bowl. "I need some help in here. You don't need to be following after your brothers. It's high time you learned how to make a pie crust."

She kicked at the dirt with her worn shoe, a hand-me-down from Walter, whose feet were already larger than hers. "But Jimmy and Walter are going fishing."

"That's no place for a lady." The old woman peered at Lum sternly. "I thought we talked about you wearing dresses. I'm gonna cut up them overalls and use 'em for quilting."

"But I like overalls, they gots pockets." What she didn't say was that they hid her emerging breasts.

"No more buts. Your daddy agreed it's best you dress like a young lady. Now let's get going on this pie."

After putting on a dress, Lum rolled up the overalls and put them in the back of her chest of drawers. Even if Granny didn't want her wearing them, sometimes she would dig them out, go out, and hope to slip back in without anyone noticing. Guthrie, Walter, Tommy Lee, and Jimmy didn't care what she wore, but Two Pint might tell on her just because he hated being the youngest. Since he was picked on by his brothers all the time, he wanted her, the only girl, to get in trouble. Being a girl had to be worse than being the youngest child.

In the kitchen, Granny was slicing apples. Reddish yellow peels

5

were in a circle around the white bowl that held the white chunks. She looked up when Lum came in.

"Much better." She nodded at the dress, then the dough bowl. "Don't you want to make a pie crust good as mine?"

"Yes, ma'am."

"Hands."

She held out her hands for inspection. She had washed them at the water pump before coming in, so Granny nodded again. "The secret is in the cold water. Always get water from the spring house." She handed Lum a tin cup.

Lum loved going to the spring house. Its darkness and damp walls and floors with moss comforted her. She crouched, hands on the mossy floor, and listened to the crickets' pleasant grating sound. She knew it was not chirping but their legs rubbing together. She knelt to the spring and let some fresh water stream into her cup. Holding it carefully, she backed out of the little shack.

After dribbling the right amount of water into the flour/lard mixture, Lum dusted her hands with flour, then rubbed flour on the rolling pin.

"Now roll your pin over it this way a few times, then the other way." Granny stood behind Lum and watched her. "I can tell this is going to be a good one. When you start patting it out you can know if it'll act right or not." She put her hands on Lum's shoulders. Lum wanted to step backwards into her grandmother's body, to feel her warmth. When she was younger, her grandmother had been very affectionate, but when Lum started "developing" as her granny said, both Granny and Daddy had stopped hugging and touching her. She didn't remember her mother, who'd died giving birth to Two Pint when Lum was not quite four. She couldn't stop blaming Two Pint for that. She knew she wasn't the kind of girl Granny wanted because she liked to do things with her brothers. They'd race and of course Tommy Lee would win, but sometimes she beat Walter, who was a year younger.

This was going to be a good piecrust, she could tell. She had made one before and it wouldn't stick together so she added more water, but it was too far gone, there was nothing she could do to save it. A piecrust either behaved or it didn't. After that first attempt, she stuck to biscuits or cobblers and left piecrusts to Granny. But now she fitted the pie pan over the dough and cut around its edges, and Granny stepped away to add sugar to the apple slices. Next came the tricky part: she had to lift the dough with the pie pan on top, flip it, and tuck the dough into the pan without it coming apart. It slipped a little but she coaxed it into place and set it before Granny's bowl of apple mixture. "All ready," she announced.

"Good girl." Her grandmother gathered the cut-away pieces of dough on a flat pan, sprinkled them with sugar and cinnamon, and placed the pan in the oven next to the pie. They'd pull it out soon and enjoy the scraps of cooked dough while they prepared dinner.

Lum Goes to Smiley's

1933

Al bounded up the back steps two at a time, slinging open the torn screen door so hard it slammed against the house. "Come on, Kenny, I smell ham." He stopped abruptly. "Lum! I wasn't expecting you so soon. Glad to have you, of course." Margaret's husband was a short, energetic man. His thinning brown hair, combed back, barely covered his sun-freckled scalp.

"I swan, Al, you're looking more and more like your daddy." Lum stared at his balding head. "Been working hard?"

"Always. I reckon you heard that storm last night. One of Moe's bulls got struck by lightning and fell on my fence. Then my bull saw the opening and got out."

A lanky, dark young man stooped to enter. "You know Kenny Doyle, Lum?" Al asked.

"I don't think we ever met."

Kenny held his hand out to Lum, who shook it vigorously. Kenny's curious eyes rested on her thick thumb. Lum wondered what he'd heard.

Al grabbed the iced tea pitcher and gulped down a glassful. "The fence is taking longer than I thought. I gotta get some more barbed wire. I'll fix that old Angus. Took us half the morning just to get him in the pen."

Margaret walked toward the table, her hair sticking out in all directions. "Al, Lum made some red-eye gravy to go with her famous biscuits."

"Umm, um! Lum, it ain't the same without you. Me and Kenny been

9

stuck with Margie's cooking." He ducked as Margaret swung at him, laughing. "One day she tried to make biscuits. They were so flat Caleb asked his Mama what it was when she put one on his plate. She got so mad, she threw that hard old biscuit at him, 'bout put a hole in the wall where it hit. Could'a killed the boy."

Margaret slapped his muscular arm. "That's a pack of lies! I did not throw the biscuits at Caleb, I was throwing them in the garbage."

"Lum could teach you, couldn't you, Lum? Can't be that big a secret. Lots of women make good biscuits for their families, don't they, Kenny?"

Kenny's mouth was full of ham and mashed potatoes. "It's all good to me. That crap they slop out in the joint ain't fit for rabid dogs."

"Lum, I bet you'd like to go to town with me, huh?" Al asked.

"Wouldn't mind." She started gathering dishes off the table. "Let me help clean up first."

Al wiped his forehead with his sleeve. "Come on out when you're done."

After washing the dishes, Lum climbed into the pickup, gathering her skirt around her.

"Been a while since you gone to town?" Al asked.

"Oh, yeah. You know how Jimmy is. He don't like being around folks if he can help it. It'll be nice to have a change of scenery." She also didn't like to be around people, although she'd feel safe with Al. But she really wanted to go with him in case he'd stop at Smiley's place. Maybe the junk man would have something she'd like.

When they reached the small town of Granite Falls, Lum stayed in the truck while Al went to the lumberyard. Al tossed a bale of barbed wire in the truck bed and started the truck. When they reached the pharmacy, he turned to her with a familiar, questioning smile. "Can you pick up some paregoric for me at the pharmacy? You know how that druggist is."

"Sure, Al."

He peeled off some dollar bills. "See how much they'll give you."

Lum pulled in her shoulders as she warily entered the store. She browsed the dry goods aisle, making her way to the back, where Mr. Reeves, feather duster in hand, stood behind the counter. Neat rows of various jars and bottles lined the shelves behind him.

"Hello, Lum. Long time no see." The white-haired pharmacist stopped dusting. "What can I do for you?"

"I need to pick up some paregoric."

"Oh, you do, huh?" He squinted toward the front window. "Looks like Al Lewis's pickup. You wouldn't be back at the Lewises' now, would you?"

"Yes, that's right. Their baby can't digest her mama's milk. A bit of paregoric works wonders with a baby's upset stomach, you know, Mr. Reeves."

"I reckon you know what you're talking about. Don't you let ol' Al get into this, you hear?" He pulled a cobalt blue bottle off the shelf.

"Yes, sir, Mr. Reeves. I'll keep a close watch on it." She paused. "It's a long drive out here, and Al's so busy, I don't know when I can get a ride again. Two bottles would last a lot longer. That baby can be awfully fussy."

"Now, Lum, there's regulations. I can't be handing out paregoric left and right."

"Oh, I'd never ask you to do anything that would get you in trouble. I guess we'll have to put up with all that crying and carrying on."

"Just this once," he sighed, slipping two bottles into a paper sack. "Two dollars."

Lum paid quickly and turned to leave. Three teenage boys stood giggling by the comic books. As she passed, a rotund blond boy whispered "morphydite." The other two sniggered. She walked by with her head held high, eyes straight ahead, and hurried into the waiting truck.

"He's on to you, but I told him it was for the baby."

"Thanks, you're a pal."

A trail of fencing rode up and down the hills, cutting through the farmland. Small hand-lettered signs surrounded by black-eyed Susans and Queen Anne's lace advertised tomatoes, squash, honey, apple cider, and peach wine. Al wasn't slowing down, so Lum realized she'd have to ask. "Al, you mind stopping at Smiley's a bit?"

"Sure thing. It'll have to be quick. I could spend hours looking at his stuff." Al pulled off the highway and Smiley strode toward the truck. Large freckles sprinkled his broad nose, spilling across caramel-colored cheeks.

"Howdy, folks." He opened the door for Lum.

"Hello, Smiley." Lum had known Smiley for most of her life. Five years younger than Lum, he'd accompanied his mother, the washer-woman, to their farm. "How's your aunt and uncle?"

"They be doing fine," Smiley said, and then whispered, "Miz Lum, I got something to show you. Something you'll like." A gold tooth shone beneath his short upper lip. He motioned for her to accompany him to a shotgun house with random remnants of paint on buckled pine siding.

Lum followed Smiley through the house crowded with furniture, paintings, vases, and stacks of boxes, weaving her way through each room, taking care that she didn't knock anything over. In a pantry off the kitchen, Smiley reached through canned tomatoes to retrieve a small package wrapped in paper. "Been saving this just for you, ma'am, uh-huh, sure have." Smiley nodded, looking pleased with himself. "Look here." He flipped the package onto her palm. Lum unwrapped the slick paper and fanned out a short stack of postcards. Smiley shifted from one foot to the other. "Look at that one, I know you'll like it." He pointed with a tobacco stained finger. "Those twins. Daisy and—who's the other one?"

"Violet," she whispered, her tongue lingering on the sound. Siamese twins, their hair in ringlets, stood in front of an obese woman whose ample flesh folded over itself. Her arm was slung over the shoulder of a bearded lady. Lum's heart quickened. With trembling hands, she wrapped the cards and said, "I'll take them all."

"Since you're such a good customer, I'll only charge you five cents."

Lum dropped the package in a large square pocket sewn on her apron, and pulled a balled up handkerchief from between her breasts.

Smiley reached into the pantry, pulling out a glass jar. "How about some chow-chow?"

Lum's eyes widened. "Ummm. Sure, I'll get a jar. How much?"

"Nickel." He winked. "Can't go out of here empty-handed."

Lum fished a dime out of the handkerchief.

"Thank you, ma'am, it's always a pleasure. I'm keeping my eyes open for any of them pictures."

She and Smiley made their way back along the circuitous trail to the front door.

Al was busy at the tables created by ancient warped doors spanning sawhorses. He held a wooden-handled drill and was digging through a box of tools, fishing lures, and all sorts of rusting objects. "Got any bits to go with this, Smiley?"

"Sure do. Can't directly say where, but there's three of 'em." Smiley craned his neck to survey the tabletops and reached across Al to grab a cigar box. He scooped out three rusty drill bits. "Now you sand those down, they be good as new, yes, sir. Anything else you can't do without?"

"I seen that sign for peach wine. You got anything a little stronger?"

Smiley grinned, nodding slowly. "Yep. You want a snort?"

"You bet!" Al answered.

The men disappeared around the house. Lum looked at the jars of honey and preserves. She wished she'd noticed whether Margaret needed any honey. She sat in the pickup flipping through the postcards. She looked for a long time at the Alligator Boy, a thin man with webbed feet and rough hands sticking out of a puckered brown suit two sizes too small. She tried to read his face, his thoughts. Pondering a handsome young man on a sturdy chair, his left leg crossing his right, wearing fine lace-up boots, she shuddered. Protruding from his side was a shorter misshapen leg with a matching trouser leg and a mismatched shoe.

When Al appeared clutching two paper bags, Lum folded the oilpaper over the cards and hid them in her pocket.

"Had to get something for Kenny, too," Al explained, climbing in the truck. "Oh, you got some chow-chow. Margie hates it, so I never get any. My mama used to make the best chow-chow."

"She sure did." Lum leaned back, patting her pocket with the new cards.

Lum plodded through the mud to the porch, where Al's twelve-year-old son, Caleb, sat in the swing, his spindly legs dangling. He stood when Lum ascended the steps.

"Come give your Aunt Lum a big hug, boy."

"Hey, Aunt Lum." He offered his cheek.

"Well, aren't you the big boy? Not too big to gimme a hug, are you?"

Caleb's arms hung limply while Lum hugged him. She remembered how he used to run into her outstretched arms and she would lift him up and cover him with kisses.

Al yelled out the truck window, "Go open the gate for me, son."

"Yes, sir." Caleb trotted ahead of his father's truck, Al driving two feet behind him.

Lum walked around the porch to the small room. She dragged the valise from the corner and lifted it onto the narrow bed. Sitting beside it, she unclasped the lock and flipped through the yellowed, brittle pages of clipped newspaper stories telling tales of "Four-Year-Old Boy Mauled by Tiger at Zoo," "Two-Headed Pig Born in Newton County," "Woman Burns Outhouse with Husband in It." She pulled some postcards from under the newspaper clippings and slipped the new ones out of her pocket. Quickly, she turned to the Siamese Twins. This was her fourth card with Daisy and Violet, but the first with a bearded lady too; this was surely the prize of her collection. She had pictures of other whiskered women, but this card was different. She imagined a family of carnival people, loving each other as their real families couldn't. Roughly rubbing her chin, she wondered what it would be like. Lum looked for her card with the twins at the Georgia fair, another with them holding musical instruments, and one with the girls in striped bathing suits on a paddle boat. She placed those on the quilt next to the new one. Next, she fanned out the cards until she found one with a bearded lady on stage, a cigar protruding from her ruby lips. She spread the other cards with bearded ladies in the adjoining tattered fabric rings. Flipping through the new cards, she caught her breath when she saw the shapely figure of the Dog-Faced Girl in a high-necked velvet Edwardian dress with a furry animal head. She didn't quite look like any dog Lum had ever seen, maybe more like a monkey. But so attractive, somehow. This card felt thicker than the others. Lum ran a fingernail along the side and realized that another card was stuck to it. Separating the cards, Lum suddenly dropped the Dog-Faced Girl. "All man, all woman, all nude," proclaimed a banner stretched across a tent. Alone on stage, arms slightly outstretched, was a slender person with small breasts and a tiny pink penis, barely covered by cloven lips.

A bitter taste came up her throat as a memory came back.

Lum kicked, blinded by the dress they'd pulled up over her head. Part of the skirt was stuffed in her mouth. Tommy Lee tightened his grip on her ankles, holding them wide apart.

"I want a look," Two Pint wailed.

"You're too young," Jimmy snapped. "Keep her mouth covered."

Walter and Guthrie held her wrists. "She got a wiener, small like a baby," Jimmy reported to his brothers.

"I told you she's like a boy," Walter taunted.

Lum screamed into balled-up cotton. Her body bucked furiously, flailing her arms and legs in the hay. The boys, unable to restrain her, ran out of the barn laughing.

She scooped up the postcards from the bed and reluctantly put them in the valise, knowing the family would be ready for supper soon. "There will always be a place for you, Lum." Her grandmother's words echoed through her thoughts. But where? Like a broom in the corner—used, then put back? Members of her family considered her useful until she overheard too many arguments or the mother became jealous of Lum's closeness to the children.

She loosened the top three buttons of her dress, spread the collar wide, poured shaving powder into a teacup and added water from the pitcher. After lathering her neck, she scraped a straight razor through the coarse hair. Wisteria, snaking through the rotted window frame, cast a long shadow across the ceiling. Abandoning the careful shaving of her chin, she abruptly yanked the wiry invader, pulling more wisteria through the opening, followed by cat briar and kudzu, coiled in a cable. Lum cut the prickly briar at its entry point and hacked at the tangled vines with the razor. She drew more into her nook, slicing snarled strands until heart-shaped, oval, jagged, and yellowing leaves were strewn across the gray pine planks. Her index fingers were raw from the briars, and the razor's edge was green. The whole hand, razor and all, went into the water pitcher. She dropped the razor, swished both hands in the cool water, and splashed the green liquid across her flushed face, the taste of dinner coming up her throat, red-eye gravy and tomato.

Kenny's Story
1933

Lum stepped off the porch and paused to look over the valley, one of her favorite views. Chestnuts, firs, hemlocks, sycamores, and oaks contrasted various shades of green lit up by the rising sun. As she rounded the corner, she saw the pile of vines that she had thrown out the window. Kenny Doyle leaned against the house, flicking cigarette ashes by the mound of foliage. Quickly she looked at the window, hoping he hadn't seen in since she'd pulled down the vines, but the chinaberry's limbs were low enough to obscure the view.

"Mornin'," he called out.

"Good morning." She nodded.

"Looks like you and me, we're the only ones up." Kenny ground his cigarette out with the heel of his worn work boots.

"Reckon so." Lum pulled the crocheted shawl around her arms against the cool mountain air.

"Can't stop staring at the mountains," he said. "Missed 'em something awful whilst I was away." He rubbed his hand against the bib of his overalls where his heart must be.

She looked away from his flat chest. "Excuse me, I was heading to the henhouse."

Kenny ambled beside her. "I remember you from when I was young. Sometimes I'd see you in town."

"I know your people." When she was a child, the Doyles had seemed dirty, but now Lum realized that their olive skin was natural. Around town they were referred to as Guineas or Melungeons, but they called themselves "Portugee."

At the henhouse, Lum took a basket off a nail on the wall.

"I could hold that for you."

Tempted to resist, she decided on politeness. "Thank you." Deftly she slid her hand under a red chicken to retrieve speckled brown eggs.

"You stick your hand under that hen?" He drew back as if the hen would attack him, not her.

She cradled the eggs in her hand, savoring the warmth on a cool summer morning, then held them toward the basket, intending to slip them in, but his dark fingers brushed her hand as he took them from her, easing them into the basket hanging from his wrist. His touch lingered on her hand even after he withdrew his and the eggs were safely deposited.

"You gonna be staying here long?" he asked.

"As long as they'll have me," she replied. "Long as I'm needed," she amended. She wanted to ask him the same question, but she had been taught that it was rude to ask company when they were going to leave. He wasn't company or family, though, he was just a worker.

"Same as me. I'm hoping for a steady job. Al's helping me out, but he can't afford more than feeding me and a dollar now and then. And I gotta find a place to stay. Even my granny weren't too glad to see me after I got out of the joint."

Chickens were milling about after abandoning their roosts, so Lum gathered a few more eggs and passed them to his outstretched palm. She wanted to touch her face with the fingers that touched his, but she reached for the basket.

"I'll carry 'em in for you."

"I can carry a basket of eggs," she snapped.

He looked through a long black lock of hair. "I weren't saying you can't. Just trying to be helpful."

She sighed. "That's nice of you."

"You and me," Kenny said, "we're kind of in the same fix, ain't we?"

"I have no idea what you mean." How dare he compare himself to her.

"Well, I don't mean to offend, but neither of us have a place to call home, do we?"

This ex-con was implying that she was like him, but she had to admit he had a point. She tried to walk quickly, but he followed her into the kitchen. Would he ever let her alone?

"Just set the eggs on the table for now. I appreciate all your help."

He sat at the table and rolled a cigarette. Lum pulled open the door of the flour cabinet and cranked the handle, measuring the sifted flour into a bowl. She poured the flour and some salt and baking powder into a hand sifter, watching the fine dust drift into the dough bowl below. She could feel his eyes on her back. When she turned around, he began to speak.

"It was a accident put me in prison. Started as a joke. Me and my daddy and my brother, Early. We were going fishing at the river and saw my sister's husband down there with some floozy. Tickling her and stuff. And my sister expecting their first kid. We didn't like him no how 'cause him and his family thought they was better than us. His family in Staunton, they didn't want him marrying her." He paused to light the cigarette, and continued, his voice rising in pitch and volume. "So me and Early and Daddy, when we saw him at the river, we decided to teach him a lesson. See, we didn't mean to kill that old boy, him being the daddy of our sister's young'un and all. We asked him to come fish with us. Didn't know he couldn't swim." He took a long drag on his cigarette, and expelled the smoke in one big puff. His leg jiggled and he started talking faster. "We thought it was funny at first and kept pushing him with the oar after we tipped him outa the boat. But then it was too late. He should'a known how to swim. Who can't swim?" He licked his thumb and forefinger and put out the flame on his cigarette and dropped the stub into a small tin holder. "Nobody's gonna two-time no sister of mine carrying a baby!" He gripped the cigarette holder so hard his knuckles paled.

Lum turned away, put a dollop of lard into the flour mixture and cut it in with two knives. When it reached the consistency of mill-ground corn meal, she poured in some buttermilk, stirred it briefly, and spread the dough on the board. With floured hands she pulled the dough toward herself, then pushed it away with both palms. She knew exactly how many times to knead it so the biscuits would rise up just right and not be heavy. She couldn't wait to slather some butter on the warm biscuit. Butter made the biscuit. Peach preserves or honey enhanced it, but butter, that made a biscuit.

Kenny's voice rose up behind her. "I weren't but fifteen when the accident happened, so I was in the boys' reformatory. Early and Daddy, they went together to prison. I din't even see 'em for three years—'til I got sent to Petersburg, where they was. Since I was young, I got out first. Soon's I got out, I went back home. Mama done died when I was gone, and Sis was living there with her new husband. I weren't welcome there, so I went to Granny and she let me in, but I know she don't want me. She said, 'I ain't gonna cook for you or wash your clothes, but you can stay here 'til you find yourself a place.' She's kinda mean." As if exhausted by the telling, Kenny slumped forward, elbows propped on his knees.

Lum remembered from her childhood the small dark woman surrounded with children, including Sampson, the only Melungeon she remembered talking to. Lum imagined his granny now as an aged woman, stubbornly holding on to the independence she earned by living long, only to have her grandson, a murderer, no less, show up as if nothing happened. Quickly she cut the dough into circles and dropped them on a blackened flat pan. *Some ham from yesterday would be good fried up with some eggs*, she thought, wiping her hands on the long apron. She couldn't help glancing over at Kenny, his head bowed with that lock of dark hair dangling. He was just trying to make friends, after all, why should she treat him like a leper?

Sampson

1907

Tommy Lee strode ahead of Lum and her brothers. Lum, Walter and Jimmy were together, trying to keep up. Guthrie had taken another route to walk with a girl. Even at thirteen, Guthrie liked girls and would like one for a while, then walk another one home from school.

Lum crunched the dried oak leaves as she walked to the schoolhouse, liking to hear them crackle. She loved school and the teacher, Miss Sanders, but none of her brothers did. They always said they weren't learning anything useful and would stop going as soon as Daddy let them.

In the schoolhouse, Walter and his friend, Al, sat together at a double desk and the other boys sat with their friends. Often no one sat next to Lum. Even though she couldn't figure out why nobody wanted to sit with her, she liked having the whole expanse of pine desk to herself. She settled in—opening up the reader, setting up her inkwell—and had a clean pad of paper in front of her when Sampson Doyle slid into the seat beside her. He had dark skin but straight hair, so he didn't look like a Negro. The Doyles rarely came down the mountain to school. They were some of the Portugee from the Knob. Most of the people she knew never went to the Knob. The Portugee didn't want people on their land, her Daddy had explained.

"I ain't got a book or nothing," he whispered.

"You can share mine," she said. Her hand was trembling. She'd never talked to one of them, and he seemed a little nervous, too.

When Miss Sanders gave them their assignment, to read a poem by John Greenleaf Whittier, she read out loud when called upon, then passed the book over to Sampson. He shook his head when Miss Sanders asked him to read the next two lines.

"Sampson, it's your time to read. Just two lines."

Lum pointed out the beginning of the line. He shook his head again. Lum realized that he hadn't come often enough to learn to read. She wished she could help him.

"Sampson," Miss Sanders said, "we're waiting."

His head dropped. Lum mouthed to her teacher, "Can't read."

"Sampson, you can't read?" Miss Sanders said.

Why does she have to announce it? Lum thought.

"If you came every day like you're supposed to, you'd be reading as well as the others."

"Sorry," Lum whispered to him. His head hung low and a lock of fine black hair covered his blue eyes.

At dinnertime, when they went home, Walter shouted, "The teacher sat Sampson Doyle next to Lum!" Their father accompanied them back that afternoon and told the teacher, "I don't care where them Doyles sit, but no Guinea's sitting next to my daughter."

So Lum went back to the double desk, fearing what she would do when Sampson came back. Miss Sanders asked him to sit at her own desk and taught the rest of the afternoon standing. Sampson wasn't there the next day or the next or ever again, even though Lum looked for him, wanting to say, "I didn't tell. I don't mind you sitting by me."

Mighty Fine

1933

The churn was between Lum's legs as she sat on the porch turning cream into butter. The far mountain ridges were as gray as the sky. Dark green evergreens offered a contrast against the hues of elms, beeches, oaks, and dark walnuts. She remembered when the woods were full of chestnuts with their yellow burrs and that sickeningly sweet smell in spring. But only a few remained here and there. The leaves would be more colorful soon. The cool weather of fall energized her, but she still had a month of hot afternoons before then. She noticed two men in button-down shirts walking along the ridge. What were they doing here? She didn't recognize them as town folks. One of them waved as they approached her.

"Good morning, ma'am." The man who had waved took off his hat, revealing a bald head with a fringe of graying hair. His shirtsleeves were rolled up to his elbows and he wore scuffed work boots.

"Good morning," she replied, waiting for them to identify themselves.

"We didn't mean to bother you. We're not from around here. I'm from Richmond, and Mr. Shapiro, here, came all the way from New York. Oh, sorry, my name's Gerald Isom."

"Pleased to meet you." City folks. What in the world . . . ? "What brings you out this way?"

"Just looking around right now. Enjoying the beautiful landscape," Mr. Shapiro said in a thick accent. She supposed that was how people from New York talked. His shirt looked freshly pressed, and his shoes still had a shine although dark earth clung to their soles. Not the kind of shoes to be worn traipsing around the mountain. His dark hair was neatly parted on one side.

"This here's one of the best views in the mountains," Lum boasted. "Least the best I've seen, although I admit I ain't gone many places."

"You folks have some mighty fine property," Mr. Isom said.

"Well, thank you, but it's not mine. My cousin's place."

"Albert Lewis," Mr. Shapiro said, looking at a clipboard.

"Yes," Lum said. "How did you . . . ?"

"We have copies of the property records," Mr. Shapiro interjected. "Well, we'll be going now."

"Thank you for your hospitality," Mr. Isom said. "I see why you like sitting out here."

What hospitality? She hadn't offered them a drink or even asked them to sit down. But they seemed anxious to leave. As if they'd taken a look, seen what they had to see, and didn't want to stay long enough to take it all in.

"You should come back in October to see all the colors, you want to see it at its best."

Mr. Isom nodded, and he and Mr. Shapiro walked down the path to High Ford Road, where Lum supposed their car was parked. What had led them up here?

She looked again at the various shades of late-summer green. As a child she had spent time here, running down the hills with her brothers and Al when they came to visit Al's family. Al and her brother, Walter, had been friends for as long as they'd known each other. In school, they had gotten in trouble more than all the rest of the kids of the seven grades put together. When she was a teenager, Al liked to tease her, along with her brothers, calling her "freak show," until Jimmy caught him doing it. Jimmy was two years older than Al and Walter, and he'd grabbed Al's overalls and hung him from a tree branch by one strap. She smiled at the memory. The next time Walter called her a freak show, Al told Walter to shut up. That didn't stop Walter and Guthrie and Two Pint from teasing her at home when Granny couldn't hear them, though.

"Mighty fine day to be sittin' on the porch, ain't it?"

Lum looked away from the valley and toward Smiley's voice. His mule, Annabelle, hitched to the wagon, was tethered to the wire fence.

"Good morning, Smiley," she called out. "What you got in the wagon?"

"You wanna have a look-see?"

"Sure." Lum draped a cloth over the churn and stood. Her knees were sore from so much sitting. She flexed her legs a few times and walked toward the wagon.

"I just got some preserves: strawberry, blackberries, figs."

"Oh, I'd love me some fig preserves." She looked at the things piled up, including pink embossed glass plates, table covers, and wooden spoons in a chipped milk pitcher, and lots of glass jars. "Got any honey?"

"Only a few jars. Haven't been all the way up to the Honey Man's to get more, but I aim to soon."

"Well I best get some now even though we still have honey from the store. Kind you got is better than from town."

"Know what else I got? Scuppernongs!" He tapped a metal washtub with his thumbnail.

"Oh, I should get some. I love to suck on 'em." She hated the bitter skins that had to be spit out. Why was it that tasty things often came in disagreeable coverings? Like honey. Who was the first person to discover that you could get something sweet from a beehive?

"You get you something to keep 'em in. I haven't had a chance to put 'em in smaller batches."

"Let me go inside a minute. I'll be right back."

In the kitchen, she saw Margaret slicing yesterday's ham into thick chunks.

"You done churnin'?" Margaret asked.

"Almost." Lum looked into the corner cabinet for a bowl. "Smiley Hawkins is here with some scuppernongs. I'm looking for a bowl to put them in."

Margaret swatted at a fly. "You wash 'em up real good, now. You don't know who touched them."

"All right." Lum paused. "Margaret, he's got some honey and figs. You have some coins?"

"Lum, we got honey."

"But not a lot. Mountain honey is better than what they sell in the store."

"I wouldn't mind some fig preserves, but don't let's get no more honey until we run out."

"But I already told him I want some."

"Tell him you don't want it. You don't owe that nigra nothing."

"It's not right to say you want to buy something, but then not do it." Lum walked to her little room and grabbed her handkerchief full of change. Back outside, she saw Smiley rearranging things in his wagon.

"I just picked up some toys Uncle Brother—I mean, the Reverend— carved." The Reverend Zachariah was well-known as a carver of spoons and toys.

"Oh, did you? Baby Meg might like one," Lum said.

"I got dogs with moveable legs, chickens, roosters, cats . . ."

"I reckon she'd like a toy chicken."

"Let's take a look. Now, here's a red ol' rooster."

"She's scared of the rooster. She might like a chicken better."

"Uh-huh. I got just the thing for your baby girl. It ain't been painted, but it been sanded down so good she won't get no splinters."

Lum felt the smooth brown chicken, wondering if Meg was old enough for the toy or if she would try to chew on it. Lum decided to keep it and give it to Meg when she was a little older. She said, "How's Hilda 'n 'em?" She hadn't met Hilda but she knew Smiley was sweet on her.

"Ornery as ever. If she was ever nice to me, her nose might fall right off."

Lum laughed. "You ever get a card with a noseless woman on it?"

"Just two flat holes above the mouth? That's like the Snake Woman, ain't it?"

She would have to go take a look at her Snake Woman card, because she couldn't remember the nose. Smiley didn't look like he was enjoying the laugh, but he often joked about how prickly Hilda could be.

"Things all right, Smiley?"

He sighed. "Will be, I think. I'm working out a plan in my mind, but I ain't ready to talk about it yet. After things work out, I'll tell you all about it." He pulled on his upper lip.

"All right." He liked to appear happy-go-lucky, but she knew better. When he was worried, he pulled on his short upper lip. He'd tell her when he felt like it. "Now I'm gonna pay you for all this." She poured coins into his pale palm. Money was scarce, and she hoped she could earn some soon. Often when she stayed with relatives she didn't have a chance to earn money, but also didn't have much opportunity to spend it. Seemed like any extra money she came by ending up going to Smiley.

"You gonna love that honey. It's so thick and dark, just the way you like it."

"I can't wait to put some on a biscuit. Margaret's worrying me about this butter, so I better get back to churning."

"Alrighty. If I get back this way soon, I'll stop by."

Lum hoped the next time he'd have a card or two for her.

First Card

1916

When Lum was young, Smiley's mother, Dessa, would help Lum's granny with the washing. A few times she brought Smiley along to play with Two Pint and whispered to Lum, "Don't let nothing happen to my boy." He'd follow after her, telling fantastical tales about seeing a talking turtle or a cat that turned into a little girl. Granny found her playing with Smiley and said, "White girls don't take care of colored children. And you're too old to be playing with him." But when Lum knew her grandmother couldn't see them, she listened to his yarns.

Then Dessa got sick and Smiley went to live with his Aunt Myrtle and Uncle Zach, a railroad porter who preached whenever he was home on a Sunday. By then Lum was in high school and she more or less forgot the little boy with tall tales. But one book she'd taken out of the school library, *Alice in Wonderland*, reminded her of him. It looked and sounded like a long Smiley story.

One day, when she was in high school, he came to the farm to show her a postcard of a long-necked woman wearing a scaly-looking outfit, the Snake Woman. He said, "See, my stories could happen."

She held out her hand and he placed it in her palm. She peered at it, trying to figure out how the Snake Woman made herself look so much like a snake.

"That's how she really is," Smiley said.

"Some folks are born looking like a snake?"

"Sure are, uh-huh."

So she wasn't the only one who wasn't normal. Born funny. "Can I have it?"

"I just wanted you to see it. I remember how you liked my stories even when my mama told me to quit telling tales."

He'd brought it all this way to show it to her? "Can I please have it? I'll trade you." She thought for a moment. "I'll trade you my lucky buckeye." That was how much she wanted evidence.

"Let me see," he said, pulling on his upper lip.

"Wait here." She ran to her room and carried the buckeye from her jewelry box, where she kept her mother's thin wedding band, a strand of paste beads, and a flattened penny that Jimmy had put on the railroad tracks.

Her first postcard. When Walter saw it, he started calling her "freak show." Even though she hated being called that, she became interested in folks called "freaks." But she never showed another card to anyone. It was her and Smiley's secret.

Late Night

1933

Meg was curled up in Lum's lap, giving her thumb a good workout. Caleb pushed some cold field peas around his plate with a piece of cornbread.

"Go on an' finish your supper, honey. Your daddy must be running late." Standing by the window, Margaret glanced at Caleb and then back outside again, cupping her face against the glass.

"I ain't hungry," Caleb complained.

"A growing boy like you? No wonder you're shooting up like a stalk of corn. We gotta put some meat on those bones or you'll fly right away." Lum shifted the sleepy baby.

Caleb slumped, long legs stretched under the pine table. "Y'all acting like you're both my mamas, and ain't neither one of you."

"Why don't we make up some plates and keep 'em warm on the stove?" Lum suggested.

"I'm so worried." Margaret turned around. "He goes out at night sometimes, but not 'til after supper. He don't never miss a meal if he can help it."

"I'm sure they'll be in directly." Lum stroked Meg's head with long fingers.

"Caleb, be sweet and put Meg to bed, will ya?" Margaret asked.

"All right." He pushed back the chair noisily, gathering his legs to stand, and scooped the baby from Lum's lap. When Caleb left the room, Margaret sat across from Lum.

"What I don't understand is why cain't one woman ever be enough for her man? Why's he always gotta go looking for another?"

"Now you don't know that." Lum didn't want to get into a dispute between Al and Margaret. It never turned out well for the third person.

"A wife knows." Margaret studied the hem of her apron.

"What makes you think he's carrying on with somebody?"

"Woman's intuition. He says he's gonna carry Kenny home, but he don't come back for hours and hours. Then he comes in stinking like a still. Those women up where Kenny lives, not a one of 'em thinks anything at all about having a baby without marrying."

"Maybe him and Kenny are visiting that ol' moonshiner."

"Then how come he just comes to bed, turns over, and goes to sleep?"

"Does he know you're still awake?" Lum asked.

"I don't get no sleep not knowing where he's at. I ask him where he's been, and he says he's too tired to talk and curls up around hisself. Wasn't like that before Meg was born."

"He works hard, no wonder he's so tired."

Margaret sighed. "I should'a knowed you'd stick up for him."

"I've known Al all my life, Margaret, like I've known you." But Margaret was a lot younger than Al. She was born when Lum and Al were teenagers. Margaret was her blood kin, but Al was almost like a brother.

"I want him here with me at night. That too much to ask?" She wandered to the window again. "He ain't even ate yet."

Lum piled chicken and vegetables on two white plates and covered each one with a glass pie pan, one for Al and one for Kenny, before placing them on the cast iron stove. She didn't know that Kenny would be with Al, but just in case, she wanted to make sure he had a good supper. Settling back down, she closed her eyes, deciding to wait with Margaret.

"I see lights shining up the hill," Margaret exclaimed.

Lum jolted, unaware she'd drifted off. She stood by Margaret, seeing nothing but a roving light rounding the last curve before the farmhouse, then she heard a loud motor, followed by the slamming of doors. The screen door squeaked open, revealing Al and Kenny.

"Glad you're still up," Al called out. "I'm starving." He kissed Margaret on the lips.

"Where y'all been?" Margaret asked.

Al's shoulders drooped. "Where haven't we been?"

"We kept your suppers warm," Lum said. "Go on and sit down. You too, Kenny."

The two men dug into the food. Margaret draped her arms around Al's neck from behind him and rested her chin on his head. He patted her arm and continued chewing.

Kenny wiped some cornbread crumbs from his mouth. "It all started with me and Al going to the sawmill to get some posts, and I asked if they had any jobs. Bobby Lee told us he ain't hiring, and the government bought the sawmill 'cause a road's gonna be built right where the mill's at."

Margaret looked puzzled. "What they putting another road up there for?"

"It's not another road, they're gonna widen High Ford Road," Al explained. "You know how Roosevelt's trying to make jobs for folks, and he's started the CCC for people don't have no jobs?"

Lum nodded. "I read about it in the papers."

"Bobby Lee said they started a scenic highway coming all the way up here from North Carolina. Like the Skyline Drive, but longer. We got to thinking maybe Kenny could get a job working on the road, so Bobby told us who to talk to and where to find him, so we drove on down to Roanoke and sure enough they hired Kenny. He's gonna be working on that road."

Lum beamed at Kenny. "That's good news." She knew he needed work. And he appeared obliging. But she couldn't forget how he said his brother-in-law needed to be taught a lesson.

"My, my," Margaret said. "So that's where y'all been all this time?" She sank into a chair.

"Oh, we ain't told the half of it," Al went on. "So we're riding down the highway when all of a sudden, Kenny says, 'What's that mule doing by the road?' Well, it's Smiley Hawkins's mule and cart. Annabelle's a-braying and carrying on something awful. We didn't see Smiley at first, so we pull over and there's Smiley laying in the dirt."

"Oh no!" Lum covered her mouth. "Was he?" She didn't dare say "dead."

"We managed to get him in the truck bed 'cause he can't move his leg."

Lum started for the kitchen door. "You left him out in the truck?"

"Hold on, Lum, he ain't out there." Al grabbed her arm. "His wagon was full up with furniture. But we figured his leg might be broke so we got some quilts from his wagon and made a right comfortable bed for him in the truck. Kenny got in the wagon and followed me to Smiley's place. That woman of his was there, and she said to leave the mule to her and get Smiley straight away to the colored midwife." Al pulled some crispy skin off of the chicken breast and popped it in his mouth.

"Amy." Lum remembered going to her for herbs from time to time when her granny's home remedies didn't work.

"That old herb woman, I thought she was gonna swoon seeing him all busted up, but she got ahold of herself and put him up in her bed. She promised she'd tend to him, so we come on home." He wiped chicken grease off his fingers with the edge of the tablecloth.

"Was he talking?"

"Moanin' more like. I think he'd been knocked out, 'cause he wasn't saying much and couldn't walk at all."

Margaret said, "I knew there was a good reason you was out so late."

Kenny's Uniform
1933

Cleaning wasn't Lum's strong suit. She preferred cooking and taking care of children, especially babies. Washing dishes, that was all right, but sweeping and mopping were not her favorite jobs. Margaret didn't care much for cleaning either, so Lum would sweep when nothing else needed to be done. She didn't like how Margaret lay down so much instead of working. There didn't appear to be anything wrong with Margaret. Lum decided she was just plain old lazy.

Today there was a crispness of early autumn. After breakfast, Lum brought the broom outside to sweep the front porch and knock down cobwebs. She was pulling the sticky strings off the broom's bristles and then trying to get them off her fingers when she saw Kenny walking toward the house. She wiped the webs on her apron and ran her dust cloth over the warped planks of the swing. It was so rough that she decided to ask Al for some sandpaper so that anyone who swung wouldn't get splinters.

"How do, Miss Lum," Kenny called out. He had on brown pants and a matching shirt and heavy shoes. It looked like a uniform. She'd liked the army uniforms that her brothers had worn. There was something about a man in a uniform. "I'm going to work and thought I'd stop by."

"I think Al's in the pasture." She waved her hand in the direction.

"I don't know I have time to go out there. I just like this farm so much. How it sits on this hill where you can see the town below."

"Me too." She paused. "Kenny, I've been wondering . . . how you came to work here?"

"Al helped me out. I just gotten outa jail and I din't want to stay up on the Knob no more. Nobody's got nothing up there, they just hunt and do a little growing and stuff, gathering sang and whatnot. My Daddy taught me and Early how to spot sang leaves practically from the time we could crawl. Soon as I walked I had a gun in my hand. I loved my life, but now, with Daddy and Early gone, it's not the same. Don't get me wrong, I love the Knob and the folks, but I wanted me a job."

Lum motioned toward the porch swing. "Want to sit a spell?"

"Yeah, for a minute." He sat, and after a short hesitation, Lum sat beside him. The swing pushed back against her weight and Kenny put his toe down to stop it. Once she was settled in, he lifted his boot and the swing went forward. They sat still and the swing slowed, then stopped.

"I went to the feed mill looking for work. That man said he didn't need me, to never come back. Al was at the mill getting a load of feed, and I started helping him throw the sacks in his truck, and he said would I come help him unload. So I come back with him, and we put some of the feed sacks in the barn, then we rode around the pasture putting feed in the troughs. He drove and I rode in the back to dump the feed. He give me a dollar and said to come back the next day. So that's how it started."

His leg was touching Lum's and she didn't pull away. She tried to think of another question to keep him there a little longer.

"I better shove off," he said, not moving.

"How you like the road work?"

"It's hard. Breaking up rocks and such. We're gonna make High Ford Road wider so more cars can come up it."

"What for?"

Kenny shrugged. "Somebody thinks folks will want to drive through the mountains. For fun."

She had to admit it was beautiful, but there was no destination except people who lived higher up than Al and Margaret—some share-croppers, the Honey Man, and finally, at the very top, on Hopkin's Knob, the Melungeons. She wondered when he had to get to work, but didn't want to ask or he might get up. Did he come to see her? Just for now she'd enjoy his company, his fresh sweat smell and the warmth of his leg against her.

Warning

1909

G ranny led the way through the woods. Feeling caught, Lum stopped to pull a blackberry vine from her shoe. A tiny drop of blood appeared where it scratched her ankle. Granny bent a branch of a mulberry tree. "Now pick the ones that aren't quite ripe. See that 'un that's half-black and half-red? It's perfect for jelly."

Lum put several half-tone berries in the bucket she was carrying. Her grandmother said, "Go ahead and eat them dark ones if you want." She handed one to Lum and they both ate the deep purple berries and spit out the stems. They climbed higher, looking for another mulberry tree. In a clearing, Lum looked up at the top of the mountain where there was a round hump.

"Don't ever go up to that Knob," Granny warned. "That's where them Melungeons live. And if you ever see them, go the other way."

"Why?" Whenever she saw them in town they kept their heads down as they walked. They didn't seem threatening. She looked amongst them for Samson, but she couldn't remember what he looked like. Most of them had very dark skin, but they were talked about differently than the colored people who were mostly sharecroppers.

Her grandmother peered at her then reached out her hand, grabbing her arm tight.

It hurt and Granny didn't let go. "They'll snatch you up and you'll never be seen again. You'll be married to one of them dirty men without nothing. They like white girls."

"But I'm only nine. I'm not old enough to get married." Granny dropped her hand and Lum saw a faint purple band around her arm where Granny had grabbed her.

"Then you'll be part of a big family of those rough men. You'd be scrubbing clothes in the river if they take a mind to get clean. You wanna be a dirty girl?"

Lum shook her head as she searched for mulberries. She liked the woods but now she was afraid one of the Melungeons would be looking for white girls to kidnap. Samson had seemed nice and not at all like someone who would snatch anybody. She wondered what he was doing now.

Whenever she went into town she clung close to Daddy, but still she looked for Samson whenever she saw some of his people.

Lum is Needed Elsewhere

1933

Lum's thick thumbnail traced a pod's rib, popping it open and dropping small black-eyed peas in a milky-white bowl. Meg noisily sucked Margaret's left breast.

"Aunt Lum, Aunt Lum!" Caleb rushed through the door. One strap of his overalls flapped against his chest.

"Thought I pinned up your strap this mornin'," Margaret drawled.

Frowning, he said, "Yes'm, but the other boys made fun a-me and called it a baby's pin." He spun toward Lum. "Miss Shay said to tell you her daddy got the pneumonia and can you come help him out while she's teaching?"

"I'm helping out your mama now, honey," Lum replied. She liked Liza Shay, but feared her father, Dan Shay, who was one of the richer members of town. He didn't even work in Granite Falls, but in the Waynesboro bank.

"Well, she told me to ask you."

"It'll just be for the daytime, won't it?" Margaret asked.

"Don't know." Caleb tugged at the loose strap.

Margaret turned to Lum. "Why not? School gets out by two. Me and Meg'll be fine for a day or two."

Lum didn't look forward to going into town. "I reckon I could go for a couple of hours while Miss Shay's at the schoolhouse."

"Just as long as you come back in time to make supper," Margaret said.

"Should be." Lum picked up a pea pod. "Caleb, when you get ready

39

for bed tonight, leave your overalls with me and I'll mend 'em for you. Tomorrow I'll walk to the schoolhouse with you and find out what Miss Shay's daddy is needing me for." She hoped all she'd have to do is sit while he slept.

Dew made the pasture look greener than it really was when Lum followed Caleb, both careful not to step in any cow piles. Four young steers, with a black stripe down their backs revealing their Angus paternity, were separated from the herd in a pen. Hay bales dotted the land and the valley was aglow with shades of gold, yellow, amber, and the bright green of hemlocks. Her bonnet blocked out the early morning sun.

"Usually I climb over the fence there," he pointed. "But we'll go to the back gate." His newly mended overalls had patches on the worn knees that Lum had added after stitching the detached strap. Now she noticed a good three inches between high-top boot and pants leg. At the wide gate, Caleb pulled the latch, swung it open, and hurried to close it behind Lum. She pondered what to say to the aloof boy. When younger he would chat away, telling her all about what critters he'd found by the creek or show her rocks he'd picked up. But now he seemed content to trudge along with his own thoughts.

Their shortcut brought them to a lower part of the highway, and she could see the schoolhouse set back from the road, its tin roof shining. She huffed along, frozen breath preceding her. Closer to the school, Caleb ran ahead and was sitting at the bench around the inner wall of the schoolroom by the time she got there. If he wanted to pretend they hadn't come together, she'd play along. At twelve, he probably valued friends more than family.

Liza Shay, a woman in her twenties, was writing on the large blackboard as children scampered in. A small wood stove in the corner of the room put out little heat. Lum approached the front of the room and announced herself by clearing her throat.

"Miss Lum, I'm glad you came." Liza rolled chalk in her hand. "You can help us out?"

"I'll do what I can. Margaret said she can spare me a day or two as long as I'm back by suppertime."

"That's fine. I made Daddy some soup, but his nerves are bad. Sometimes he shakes something awful and he needs help eating. That's been going on for a while, but now he's all congested. Doc Meadows says it's the pneumonia." Liza wiped her chalky hands on a piece of flannel. "You know the way from here?"

"Sure do. I'm gonna sit outside a minute to catch my breath, then I'll get going." Her toes felt cramped, and the ball of her right foot was about to come through the thinning soles of her shoes.

"Take your time. Daddy should be okay for a little while."

Lum knew if she took off her shoes her feet would hurt even more once she put them back on. She sat on a bench under an oak full of golden brown leaves. Across the highway was a field where clumps of dark workers, chained together, were piling heaps of chopped tobacco as a truck slowly made its way around the field. Whenever the truck stopped, the five or six chained men would throw the wilted leaves on the back and then walk jerkily toward the next pile. Cyrus Snell always had a group of convicts working the fields to pay off their fines that he'd paid for them. After about ten minutes of watching, Lum walked down the highway into Granite Falls.

Red-berried hedges surrounded the Shays' tidy yard. In one corner, lettuce, collards, cabbage, and spinach were planted in straight lines. All the draperies of the square blue house were closed. Lum lifted the brass frog knocker and dropped it against the door a few times. A three-day growth of gray beard peeked through a narrowly opened door. "What the hell you doing here?"

"Your daughter asked me to come look after you."

"She can look after me her own self." A bony wrist held the door, a wrinkled white shirt covered his arms.

"I'm here while she's at school."

"Why can't you watch those schoolchildren and let her care for me?"

"If you don't want me here, I'll get going. Wasn't my idea." Lum spun around, pulling her sunbonnet over her eyes, partly relieved, partly annoyed that now she'd have to walk back up the mountain.

"Not so fast. You can heat up some soup for me. Some cornbread would be nice, too. Then you can leave if you're a-wanting to." He opened the door wide. An oil lamp shone over an open newspaper spread across a horsehair sofa. He gathered up the newspaper, tucked it under his arm and headed toward the kitchen.

Lum followed him down a long hallway, looking at pictures of men in dress military uniforms. Seeing that one of them was Dan's son, Peter, she drew away, and on the opposite side of the hall, she noticed an old oval picture frame holding a wedding picture. Sun streamed through the glass-topped kitchen door, revealing dust motes in the air. While Lum mixed cornmeal, buttermilk, baking soda, salt, and egg, Dan sat reading at the end of a table covered with a lace tablecloth. She enjoyed the nearness of the icebox since Al and Margaret, like most farm families, relied on a spring house. Dan coughed into his handkerchief. He grumbled, "Roosevelt don't know what he's doing."

"I think he's off to a good start. He created that Civilian Conservation Corps so young men can get jobs." Lum lit the fire under a large pot of chicken stock.

"If they'd join the Army, they wouldn't need government programs. This is the time to sign up. Like I told my sons, we're at peace so there's no danger of going to war right now. Not like when I had to go fight the Spaniards. I got no patience with folks begging for money. Anybody knocks on my door wanting anything, I tell him to go enlist." His shirt hung limply on his chest and shoulders.

Lum stirred the pot with a long-handled wooden spoon and inhaled the fragrance of chicken, carrots, onions, and celery.

"The Army will take care of all your needs. Give you a place to live, food to eat, a good pension. Hell, they'll even bury you."

One of her brothers had been killed in the Great War, his body never recovered from overseas. Probably not enough of Tommy Lee left to bury, her daddy had said. And Peter Shay had been in college the year that three of her brothers went to war.

"I know you lost some kin in the war, but they died for a cause. It wouldn't bother me none if I'd given my life for my country." He sipped some broth, and then continued, "The shape this country's in now, Hoover drove the nail in the coffin, and Roosevelt's digging a six-foot hole." Dan's shaking hand sloshed soup down his shirtfront. "Damn! I can sit here all day without the shakes, but when I eat or drink something, my hand turns against me."

Lum picked up a linen napkin and dabbed at his shirt.

"Don't matter, nobody's gonna see me."

"You want me to help with your soup?"

"Just this once if you've a mind to."

Scooting a chair close to his, Lum dipped a spoon into the steaming bowl and blew on it as she was accustomed to doing for children. He opened his mouth, and she slid the spoon on his tongue. With the napkin she wiped his whiskered chin.

"I'm not a baby!" he growled, blue-greenish eyes boring into her.

No, babies are a lot easier, Lum thought. She looked at the clock on the mantel.

"What time does Liza get home?"

"Too late, you ask me." He coughed, a long, rasping cough, and couldn't stop. He gasped, choking for breath.

"You all right?"

He waved his hands erratically.

Lum rushed behind him, grabbed the prickly chin in one hand, placed the other on his reddened forehead, and tipped his head back toward her soft stomach. "Just small breaths, don't try too hard."

After some shallow breaths he was able to breathe. "Something got caught in my throat, like a big wad of that gunk I keep hacking up."

Backing away, Lum said, "I'll make you some licorice root tea. That'll clear you up."

"I hate licorice."

"It's not candy," she scolded. "Medicine."

"Doc Meadows didn't say anything about drinking no licorice tea."

"There's some things Doc Meadows doesn't know, and that's a fact." She pulled a gnarled root out of the square pocket sewn on her corduroy dress. She put it into a pot and added water.

He spat into his handkerchief, balled it up, and laid it by his bowl. "Think I'll lay down."

"Need some help?"

"I reckon I can get to my own bed," he snapped and pushed up from the chair. A dry cough overcame him for a few seconds, and he coughed on the thumb-end of his fist. The skin of his knuckles seemed almost transparent.

When Lum heard the bedsprings creak, she dipped a bowl of soup and sat at the newspaper. She hadn't read one while she'd been at the Lewises. After getting caught up on national news, she turned to her favorite part—local stories. A man had been stopped in Waynesboro for swerving all over the road and was arrested when his trunk revealed a large cache of moonshine and shotguns. Two women and four children were riding with him, and they stayed at a boarding house when he was put in jail, but by morning, the women and children were gone, and so was the silver flatware. She wondered how the boarders ate their breakfast.

The Washington Zoo was greeting the arrival of two African giraffes. Their graceful necks rose above the wire fence where they were confined with an elephant. Maybe someday she could take the train to Washington and visit the zoo.

She turned the page and looked at a movie ad for *Little Women*. She'd loved that book and remembered the illustrations—Jo dancing in the burnt dress, Meg entertaining her suitor on the couch, Beth on her deathbed, Amy and Laurie in a boat. How wonderful to be able to see the movie. Burnt licorice smell filled the kitchen. The water had boiled down and now the pot was blackened. She grabbed the pot off the stove to start over. At least the Shays had an indoor water line. But first she'd have to scrub the pot. She couldn't have Dan think she was dirty.

Rich Boys
1913

All through her childhood, Lum had known Peter Shay and Braxton Snell as "the rich boys." Oldest sons of powerful men. Braxton's father, Cyrus Snell, owned most of the land around Granite Falls and most of the lower part of the mountain. The Snells had come after the Civil War and bought up many of the plantations from bankrupt landowners, one by one, until they had thousands of acres planted with tobacco. Whites and blacks who were sharecroppers with tiny plots of their own worked the tobacco fields along with black convicts from three counties.

The Shays were town people who didn't farm, but who ran the town. The whole time Lum was growing up, Peter's grandfather was mayor. He'd visit their farm every four years and bring a bottle—not a jug of moonshine, but rather brown liquor that her father was very grateful to get. Peter's father, Dan Shay, was a banker; one uncle was the sheriff, and the other one was councilman. Sometimes there would be another councilman, but they were either Shays or Snells.

At school, Lum knew not to even try to talk to the rich boys. The town girls flocked to them like hungry cows at a trough, getting their weekly feed. Four years older than Lum, Peter was tall with dark hair, and the shorter Braxton had red hair, freckled skin, and translucent lashes.

Most of the farm students quit school after seven years, but Lum wanted to go to high school. Her daddy didn't want her to, but Granny said, "What's the harm? She likes learning." Except for Two Pint, who was still in grammar school, her brothers were working on the farm, so she was lonely at school. None of the other farm kids were there, and those who lived in town ignored her.

One afternoon, she was walking up High Ford Road toward home, enjoying stepping in sunlit patches that sneaked in between tree branches. Suddenly, Braxton and Peter jumped out of the woods in front of her and laughed when she reared back, startled. Braxton grabbed the sack that she carried her notebook and schoolbooks in.

"You carrying a sack of flour, girl?"

"No, my books. Give it back." She'd get a whipping if she came home without the books, and she'd probably flunk, too.

He flung the sack in a circle while she watched, mouth open.

"Whoo, watch it go," Peter said as the sack spun faster and faster without anything coming out.

Suddenly, the bag stopped, and one of her books fell out. Braxton stepped on it and ground it into the rocky soil. "You want your book?" he asked.

Too close to tears to speak, she merely nodded.

"Come here."

Peter jeered, "Whatcha gonna do, kiss her?"

Braxton wrinkled his nose, then smiled. "Yeah. Come give me a kiss, big girl, if you want your books."

"I can't," she managed to say.

"You can't?"

"No." She wanted to say, you don't like me, people only kiss people they like. And she didn't like him. Earlier she didn't have a reason not to like him, but now she did.

He pointed toward Crooked Creek. "Peter, you think I could toss this bag all the way into the creek from here?"

"Hell, no, Braxton. You might can pitch a baseball, but even you can't hit the creek from here."

"Wanna bet?"

"Yeah. If you can . . ."

"No! They're my books! Give 'em to me," Lum shouted.

He crooked his finger. "Come 'ere. One little kiss and I'll give you your flour sack and all your books. Otherwise, you'll be fishing 'em out of the creek."

Her feet felt heavy, as if they couldn't possibly move. She wished she were a tree, firmly planted in the woods, where no one would ever say, "Come 'ere." She heard that all the time at home.

Braxton swung the sack over his shoulder, as if to throw, and another book fell out. She stepped toward it, but Peter picked it up.

"Now you gotta kiss both of us," Braxton said.

Peter said, "Not me. She walks like a boy."

"Yeah, but she's got titties like Miss Irma Ray."

Lum could feel her temperature rise. Miss Irma Ray had been her daddy's teacher and was now so fat that she never left home. Sometimes when Lum went with her daddy for deliveries they'd take milk to Miss Irma Ray and she'd be sitting up in bed because she was too big for any of the chairs.

"Give me my books!"

Peter stepped forward, holding out the book, and when she reached for it he jerked it away, holding it over his head. She grabbed his arm. When she dug her fingers into his muscle, he relented. "All right, here's your book—jeez, some folks can't take a joke."

Now she had to get the bag *and* the book on the ground. "Please, Braxton," she begged.

"One kiss," Braxton said.

He wasn't giving up. What if he tried to look up her skirt like her brothers had done? But she had to get her books back. When she reached for her bag, he put both hands on her breasts and pushed her away. "Yuck! You think I want to kiss you?" Braxton dropped the sack by the book. "Come on, Peter, let that dirty thing get on home."

Lum ran to tell her daddy. Guthrie and Tommy Lee wanted to beat up Peter and Braxton, but their daddy said, "Don't go messing with them boys. They can hurt you with more than fists. You gotta choose your battles." He turned to her. "Stay away from them."

"They come out of the woods."

"You see 'em again, just keep walking, run if you have to."

This surprised her, since she'd been instructed not to run but to walk once she started looking like a woman while still a girl.

Braxton never touched her again, but she heard him bragging to other boys about feeling her breasts. The town girls, who had never been friendly before, now turned hostile, sighing loudly when Lum raised her hand and gave the right answer. They started calling her "Miss Know-It-All." She quit volunteering answers, and once her math teacher asked her to stay after school.

"Is everything all right? You turn in your homework every day, but you've gotten so quiet." Miss Campbell smelled like flowers, but Lum couldn't decide which kind.

Lum hated to disappoint the one person who had encouraged her in her studies. "The other girls . . ." Miss Campbell was a town person after all, and she favored the richer students. "I just want to give others a chance to answer."

"Don't worry about anybody but Lum. You are one of the smart farm girls. Keep up with your studies, won't you?"

"Yes, ma'am."

The teacher reached for Lum's wrist, laying her soft hand on it. "I tell you what. You don't have to raise your hand. I'll call on you from time to time so no one feels like you're showing off."

So she knew what the other girls said. Miss Campbell's pale arm, nearly hairless, was not like hers, tan from working outdoors, and with coarse dark strands of hair. She wished her body was like Miss Campbell's, and she liked the light touch. No one put their hand on her like that. "Yes, ma'am."

"Let's just get you out of high school."

I'm one of the smart ones, Lum thought. *What good will that do me?* Granny had told her she probably wouldn't marry, but she wanted to do something other than take care of the farm. Maybe she could get a job somewhere. She'd think about that and work on getting good grades.

A Little Spending Money

1933

When Liza came home, Dan was still in bed. Liza said, "Let me give you a ride back up the mountain."

Lum edged toward the door. "No, Liza, you don't need to drive me home. Stay here with your daddy. He's been sleeping since dinnertime, and he'll want more soup when he gets up." After sitting all day, she looked forward to ascending the mountain alone. With her hand on the door knob, Lum watched Liza pull a shiny black change purse from the pocketbook dangling on her wrist.

"Can't tell you how much I appreciate you coming over today. I don't want to delay you getting back to Al and Margie's. Could you come back tomorrow around lunchtime?"

"I reckon Margaret can do without me a few hours." When she saw Liza open the purse, she dropped her hand from the knob.

"Here's a little something for your troubles." Liza put two quarters in Lum's palm. After folding a handkerchief around the coins and tucking it in her blouse, Lum went out. She heard the front door click behind her and pulled the shawl around her shoulders. Looking straight ahead, she paced her steps with the breaths. She hadn't expected to get paid. Now she could buy something for supper. But that meant seeing folks.

At Fairfax Square she circled the pond. The ducks that frequented the pond had already left for the winter. Lord Fairfax's statue had a green tinge. She clucked her tongue. Town people only washed the old fellow once or twice a year. The statue showed him as a young dandy with a riding crop and high boots. His muscular legs were supposed to show leggings, but they looked like bare legs between his coat and boots. She'd heard of gangrene and imagined it as creeping green, like the color at the top of his boots.

She approached the empty building with "Stephen Harper, Attorney at Law" in faded gold lettering across the glass. Someone had started to scrape the letters but only got through the first "p" so that from a distance it looked like "hen Harper, Attorney at Law." Mr. Harper had been the only lawyer in Granite Falls until he moved to Staunton to join a large law firm. Probably not enough business in town to keep a lawyer busy. After Mr. Harper, a man who sold funeral insurance had been in that space, but he'd only lasted a year or two. Times were too hard for folks to be paying for a funeral. Most people did it the old way—wash the body, sit up with it one night, bury it the next.

Suddenly, Lum realized the office was no longer empty. Long tables were covered with rolled up sheets of paper. Large maps hung on walls. A typewriter sat on the formerly abandoned desk. Two men sat in a corner, one with his leg crossed over his knee, long leg swinging. She turned away, wondering who they were or what type of business they were in.

After Dan had gone to sleep, it had been quite pleasant, reading the newspaper without a fussy baby or dinner to prepare. Once she got back, it would be time to start cooking. Sure was nice getting a little spending money. Fifty cents! She could buy something special for supper and still have money left over for more cards the next time Smiley had some. The general store had barrels of lemon sticks, horehound, sour balls, and pickles. She could imagine the tangy taste of lemon that became sweeter the more she sucked the stick down to a sharp point.

Oak cases behind the counter held canned goods, rye and wheat flour, coffee, and sugar. At the counter stood two men she recognized as Melungeons. One was a little bent over, but the other stood erect. Two burlap bags were on the counter.

"You swear there's nothing but sang in them sacks?" Miss Bridges, a pale woman with lanky gray hair, reached her hand into the bag's opening. She had taken over the store from her father in the past year.

"Yes'm," said the man with the curved back.

"I don't take to folks a-cheatin' me."

"We swear, ma'am," the other man said. "If it ain't what we say it is, you find us and we'll make good on it. Just ask for Elias and Simon Collins. Everybody know us."

"Iffen you lie, I'm not buying nothing from none of you people." Miss Bridges lifted the sack. "Let me weigh it."

Lum stood back from the counter, trying to be invisible while scanning the rows behind Miss Bridges for the familiar red can. The store smelled of ham and sawdust. She hoped none of those troublemaking boys came in. She never knew when someone would call her names. The Melungeons never bothered her, but other than Kenny and his uncle, Samson, who she had shared a desk with decades earlier, she hadn't had much interaction with them. They kept to themselves, just as she tried to do. But their dark skin and shabby clothes made them stand out more than she did. If people didn't know her, they'd just think she was a tall, hefty woman. But the people who'd heard about her without knowing her were the ones to watch out for.

When she didn't see what she was looking for, she moved to the back of the store, away from the door. Looking out the window, she saw a group of road workers straggle across the square. They gathered around the statue in small groups. Kenny, by himself, was sprawled under a large oak. The late-afternoon sun was still high enough to provide dappled shade across his supine body. *Oh, let them move on*, she wished, not wanting to have to walk out to a bunch of men.

When the Collinses finished their transaction, Lum approached the counter.

"Excuse me." Lum cleared her throat.

Miss Bridges, back to sitting on a tall stool, slowly turned toward Lum. "What'cha want?"

"Got any salmon?" She could make a fast supper of salmon patties and some of the vegetables she and Margaret had put up in late summer. All she'd had was chicken soup, not like the big midday dinners she was used to, so she was hungry. She reckoned town people ate that way all the time, calling the noontime meal lunch.

"Sure do. How many?"

"Two."

The proprietress groaned as she stood and pulled two red-labeled cans of salmon off a shelf and placed them on the counter.

Although Lum needed shaving soap, she hated to ask for it. She was using Margaret's lye soap, but ever since Jimmy shared some of the store kind made for shaving, her skin liked it better. "Soap?"

"'S'over there." She pointed with her chin.

Four of the road men opened the door and Lum heard Elias Collins hollering, "You think you better'n us!"

Lum craned her neck to look out an open window. They weren't yelling at the road workers; Elias and Simon were standing over Kenny, who had his hand against his forehead as if to block the sun.

"Them fellas know you been to jail?" Simon jeered.

She moved to the back of the store to look for the soap. She didn't want to be noticed by these rough men. When Mr. Bridges ran the store, his stock had remained in the same place for decades, but his daughter liked to change things around. How she managed to move anything was a mystery since she was always sitting when Lum came in, and she acted bothered whenever asked for anything.

"Damn mountain wops," one of the men in the store said in a strange accent.

A sandy-haired man said, "He should go on with them others. He don't belong with us."

"Hell, I thought he was a nigger, but his hair's so long and straight," drawled a boy who looked too young to be working away from home.

"Nah, they about as lazy, but they different. Bunch of Guineas." The speaker was one of the local boys who used to tease Lum. She turned her back to them in fear that he would harass her.

"Them boys said he been to jail."

"Ha!" one man said, fingering the rim of his hat. "Bet more'n one of our gang's been to the big house." He grinned. "Not that I know for a fact."

The others laughed and joked with each other about who'd been imprisoned, but they all denied it, hanging around the front counter while Miss Bridges sliced meat and bread for them.

Lum stayed in the back corner, fearful that the teasing would turn to her. Just in case, she pulled the shawl around her neck, hiding her Adam's apple. After they left she put a bar of Colgate's Shaving Soap on the counter, hating how her hands trembled. "It's for Al," she said, then wished she hadn't. It might make Miss Bridges look at the darkness of her jaw. But Miss Bridges just told her the total and bagged the soap, along with canned salmon. More men poured in through the door as she exited.

Lum scanned the grassy square where the men from the store were eating out of white butcher paper. But Kenny was gone. Somehow she felt empty. When she had seen him under the tree alone she'd had mixed feelings, wanting to talk to him but feeling reluctant to break the solitude she craved. She hoped the Collinses didn't start a fistfight with him or hurt him in any way. But why did she care? She barely knew him. But still, there was something about him. And he got it from both ends—from his people and from strangers.

Heading down the highway, Lum passed Smiley's house, where a roughly lettered plank said "Closed Til Sundee." Blankets covered the tables. Lumps and bumps verified that his goods were merely covered up. She had a few coins left. Maybe he had some new cards for her. Wouldn't hurt to stop for a minute.

Heading for the back door, she rounded the house. She imagined folks stopping by at all times of night for liquor. At dusk, usually a lamp shone from the back, but not today. No sign of life, not even the mule. Under the shed was his wagon filled with furniture. She wandered up to it. Sure was a lot of stuff. Where was his mule, Annabelle? It'd been at least a month since Al had told how he and Kenny found Smiley hurt on the road, but she hadn't heard anything more. Who would know? Al had taken him to Amy's, so maybe he was still there. When could she manage to go to the herb lady's cabin to see him? Her eye twitched and she felt a flush of shame. Instead of worrying about him, she had thought of herself and the cards.

Lots of folks would be looking for moonshine since Smiley wasn't around, that was for sure. All her brothers had a taste for liquor. When she was young, they thought it was funny to give her some, but she got so sick she wouldn't even look at it again, let alone smell it. They laughed and said, "It'll put hair on your chest."

Boo-Hah

1908

Lum slumped over the dinner table, staring at the pork and apple-sauce on her plate. She'd been feeling queasy, and looking at food made it worse. With her eyes still on her plate, she asked, "May I be excused?"

"Aren't you hungry?" Granny looked at Lum's plate.

"I'm feeling poorly."

"Go on and lay down a bit," Granny said. "Hope you didn't eat too much of your birthday cake." They had celebrated her eighth birthday only the day before.

When she stood, Lum realized her apron was still on, tied tight around the waist. Maybe if she took it off, she'd feel better . . . but that didn't help. She'd felt sick at the stomach before, but this was different. In bed, she pulled her new bunny to her stomach, the one Granny had made for her birthday. It was made from the overalls she had loved, and the fabric was soft from being worn. Was the cloth from her seat? Her knees? She stroked its long ears, denim on the outside with a pretty floral pattern on the front part. The small red and yellow rose cloth was the scraps from her new Sunday school dress. The washerwoman's four-year-old son, Smiley, said he had a cloth doll that talked to him. What if Bunny could talk? It didn't matter, she could talk to Bunny and Bunny would listen.

"The boys said liquor would put hair on my chest and it's happened, Bunny." She put her finger through the gap in her dress front and touched the hair that grew around her nipple. It was sore. Both nipples were poking out and were often tender, but not like now. She carefully felt the swelling around the nipple and found it slightly painful when pressed. "Oh, Bunny, my buddy, my buddy bunny, I don't have anyone to talk to, not like you." When her grandmother had measured her for the red and yellow dress, Lum's nipples had been flattened by the tape and she didn't want Granny to see how swollen they were. She'd just held her breath, trying to ignore the pressure. She knew when she grew up she'd have breasts like Granny, even though Granny's settled around her waist. She hoped hers wouldn't be so long and low as Granny's. She wanted hers to be like Miss Sanders's: high and small.

She could hear her brothers in the orchard south of the house, yelling at each other, laughing, dragging ladders and wagons from tree to tree, the apples ringing in the metal bucket, then being dumped in the wagon. If she weren't in bed she'd be helping wash dishes, not picking apples. Sometimes she was glad she didn't have to do boys' work, but other times she was jealous of them working together. It was different from being with her grandmother all day. She wanted to be part of their fun.

It felt better to hold her knees as close to her chin as they would go. She'd stretch out, but the pain got worse, so she'd curl up around Bunny. After dozing for a bit, she woke up and rolled over. There was a bloodstain on the sheet. She groaned. *I'm dying*, she thought. It's like when Mama had Two Pint and there was all that blood. So much blood that when Granny put the sheet in the washtub the water turned red as a cardinal.

The blood was running down one leg, from her privates. Her underclothes were soaked. Was that where Mama's blood had come from? Maybe Granny could help with some of that nasty-tasting medicine.

"Granny," she called. "Gran-neee!" Louder, "Grannee, please help me."

Granny rushed into the room, drying her hands on the full-length apron. "Lord sakes, child, what you bellyaching about?"

"Look." With her legs apart, sitting on the bed, Lum pulled up her dress and pointed to her underclothes.

"Some boy been messing with you?"

She shook her head.

"Did you fall on something when you was out horsing around?"

"No. I woke up bleeding. Am I gonna die?"

"Oh, my little girl." Granny sat on the edge of the bed and hugged her granddaughter. "You're too young for what this looks like. I'm gonna get you a bundle of rags and safety pins to put into some clean underclothes. Give me the bloody ones."

After she balled up the soiled cloth, Granny said, "Now get you a nice dress, we're going to the doctor."

On the way to see Doctor Miles, Granny told her about her time of the month and even told her to look at the moon when it came up. It would be first quarter, Granny said, and when it was first quarter again, she'd bleed again. "If this is your time," she said. "I hope that's all it is and you're not ailin' none."

The doctor poked her private parts, ran his fingers over her swollen nipples, trailed the line of hair in the valley of her chest that picked up again on her stomach, and made her raise her arms to look at the hair growing under them. He even put his finger inside of her, reminding her of when she'd seen her daddy put his arm inside a cow having a breech birth. Finally he let her put her clothes back on.

With Lum sitting on his table, he settled into a chair and, looking only at Granny, said, "She's a girl and a boy both. She's developing both parts of herself at an early age. She's got a thing that's too small for a boy, but too big for a girl. I'd advise against marriage. No man's gonna want . . ."

A boy and girl both—how can that be? Lum wondered. *But boys don't have that time of the month.* She wanted to ask Dr. Miles, but he wouldn't even look at her.

He leaned toward Granny, his voice rising. "I never seen one before. When we learned about it in college they said it was one in a million. Never thought there'd be one out in the country." He seemed excited, as if he'd examined the Boo-Hah, the half wolf, half boar rumored to roam the hills killing lambs and baby goats. But she was a girl, not an "it." She couldn't wait to leave, to go back home and think about all this. Granny was looking at her lap, no longer paying attention to the doctor or even Lum. She pulled out some bills, and without saying anything to Dr. Miles, she hurried Lum out the door.

Lum's stomach was still hurting and she was sore from all that poking and probing. The rags were rubbing against her inner thigh. Climbing High Ford Road, she had an idea. If she was both, could she be a boy if she wanted? "Granny, what the doctor said . . ."

Her grandmother kept walking, looking straight ahead. She hadn't said a word since they left the doctor's office. Lum took a deep breath. "So I can be a boy?"

Granny stopped as if she'd hit an invisible wall. She put her hands on both sides of Lum's face. "No, you're a girl! That blood proves it." She dropped her hands and started walking even faster than before. "I never heard such nonsense in all my life! Whoever heard of a soul being two things at once? Now, more than ever, you need to act like a proper young lady. And I don't want you talking to nobody about what that durn doctor said."

The Road Men

1933

"Lord sakes, Lum, thought you'd never get back!" Margaret sat at the kitchen table, bouncing Meg on her knee. A bowl of okra was in front of her, along with sliced okra piled on one end of a cutting board.

"I got us some can salmon for dinner. Thought you-all'd like something different."

"Oh, that's kindly," Margaret said. "How's ol' Dan?"

"Mean as ever, but once I got him to sleep it was like caring for another baby." She reached for Meg, who happily left her mother's arms for Lum's. "Not like my sweet little Meggy-Meg. Nobody's sweet as my Meggy-Meg."

Meg giggled when Lum touched the tip of her pug nose.

Margaret chopped three okras at once. "I hope Al's gonna like the salmon, Lum, he's about to have a fit." With her knife, she pushed the sliced ones to the pile and pulled three more from the bowl.

"'Cause I was gone?" Lum kissed Meg's soft cheek, savoring the clean baby smell.

"Oh, don't be silly. He barely missed you even though I had to make dinner all by myself. This man was here wanting the farm."

"What?" Lum looked over Meg's head, the baby's fine hairs tickling her chin.

"That road's going right through here."

"Through here? What do you mean here?" Lum sat, settling Meg on her lap. "Kenny said they were widening High Ford Road."

"They want the farm for the road. The farm, Lum!"

"Well, I can see they want part of the pasture land since it goes right up to the road."

"They want the whole farm. They want us to sell it and move away."

"But where would we, y'all, go?"

Margaret shook her head. "This Yankee from Ohio was telling us about a factory town they're starting up for mountain people."

"They want Al to do factory work?"

"Women, too, Lum." She lined up three okras on the cutting board.

"What'll happen to me if y'all sell the farm? Do they want ours too?" Jimmy and Walter had inherited her family's farm and she spent most winters there. She never thought it would be gone. "I don't know how to do nothing in a factory."

"Don't worry, Al won't sell. He told him the land's been in his family since before Yankees had any business coming down here telling us what to do. That Yankee acted like he'd been bit by a snake. He said they needed our farm because of the flatness. They're having to blast through mountains, and our land would be a good lookout point for folks where they can park their cars and look down into the valley. Well, that didn't convince Al neither, so the man said he'd be back when Al calmed down."

"Did Al have one of his temper tantrums?"

"You know how he gets." Margaret chopped the okra, striking them harder than before.

Lum hoped Al wouldn't take it out on any of them. "He like salmon patties?"

"I don't know. Just to be safe, let's fry up some chicken. That's something I know he'll like. You and me, we can eat the salmon."

So that was what those men were doing that day, Lum realized, wandering around looking off mountains for the best view. She'd always admired the overlook, but what would it be like with a wider road winding up it? Dinner would be tense if Al had gotten all riled up, so she'd better make something special. He loved chicken gravy over biscuits, so maybe that would mollify him a bit. But she was determined to have salmon patties too, she'd been thinking about them all the way up the mountain.

"I ain' eating this." Caleb pushed the plate of salmon croquettes. "It stinks."

"You don't have to," Al said. "It's sissy food, ain't it?"

"Sissy food?" Lum was puzzled.

"No disrespect, Lum, but no man would eat it. Son, pass the plate to your mother."

"She ain't my mother."

Al stood and yanked Caleb out of his seat. "You say that one more time, and I'll blister your behind."

"Honey . . ." Margaret pleaded.

"He's gotta understand you're his mama now." Al tightened his grip on Caleb's arm.

"I love him just the same, but I can't take the place of his real mama."

Lum took a small bite of salmon. She loved the salty taste of things from tin cans.

"My boy ain't good enough for ya?"

"Honey, I didn't say that. Loosen his arm and let him eat."

Lum concentrated on eating the salmon croquettes, determined to not say anything when Al was in such a mood. She understood how it was hard for Caleb, getting a stepmother barely ten years older than himself.

"If you ain't his mama, you cain't say what I do with him."

"I'm his *new* mama. I don't want to take nothing away from his *real* mama."

"Sit down, boy." Al glared at his wife as he released his grip.

Rubbing his arm, Caleb sat and stared at his empty white plate.

"Here, Caleb, take both drumsticks." Margaret passed the plate of chicken pieces toward him. "I know they're your favorites."

"Yes, ma'am."

"Al, honey, go on and take both breasts. Me and Lum will eat the salmon croquettes."

After a few minutes of quiet punctuated by chewing noises, Al asked, "Where'd that salmon come from anyway?"

"Lum bought it at the store on the way home. She thought it would be a nice change."

"Change I don't need." He dredged his biscuit through the gravy. "Lum, what you think about this road coming through here?"

Careful, she thought. *If he wants a fight, he's not getting one from me.* "I don't know much about it."

"Damn Yankees trying to get the farm."

"You don't have to sell, do you? I mean, it's your land, they can't make you."

"Damn right I don't! They ain't getting it no way, no how."

"Good for you." She savored the salmon, the way it fell apart in her mouth.

"Somebody gotta stand up to the government, don't you think?"

"My daddy used to say to stand up for what you believe in. Then in his next breath he'd say, 'You can't fight City Hall.'"

"Your daddy was a wise man, but *I'm gonna* fight City Hall. They ain't taking the farm. Ain't gonna be no lint head."

Caleb looked up from his drumstick. "What's a lint head?"

"Them that works at a cotton mill," Al explained. "Men, women, children live their whole lives working for the mill, and they think they have their own home, but it really belongs to the mill owner. They're no better than sharecroppers living in them shacks Snell has."

"Oh, Al, it's not the same. I hear the folks working in mills have it pretty good. The owners take care of 'em." Margaret sipped some buttermilk.

"Cyrus Snell says he takes care of his workers, too, but you don't believe that, do you?"

"No, I know how he is."

"He don't take no shit neither. Look what happened to Smiley."

"Cyrus Snell the one beat up Smiley?" Lum asked. She'd suspected as much. She knew Smiley was one of the few Negroes who didn't work for Snell and that Snell hated him. Smiley had told her so.

"What I hear. He told the sheriff Smiley was carrying stolen goods."

"But his wagon's still full of furniture. How come the sheriff didn't take it?" Lum speared a piece of fried okra.

"He don't know who it belongs to." Al shrugged.

"Al, it's not true." How could he turn against Smiley and side with Snell?

"How else would a nigger get such fancy stuff?"

"I don't know. He bought it?" He had bought things from Lum, but she didn't want anyone to know about what her grandmother had left her.

"With what? You think he has money when none of us do?"

"He sure sells enough liquor to keep himself in high cotton. You know that."

"What you mean, I know that?" He glared.

Oh no, she thought, *here I was trying to not get him mad and look what happened. He is definitely spoiling for a fight.* She mustered up her innocent voice. "Nothing. It's well known. If you want anything, you go see Smiley. Anything." She paused. "Least that's what folks say." They each would keep each other's secret, even though Al didn't know what she bought from Smiley.

Al Speaks Up

1910

Lum could remember the first time any of them met Al. He was led by his sister to the one-room schoolhouse the same time Lum arrived with Jimmy and Walter. Almost the instant Al and Walter laid eyes on each other they were pals.

On Saturday, after chores, Al would come to their house, or Walter would go to Al's. It was not a short walk between the two farms, so sometimes Al's daddy would bring him in a wagon. If so, his sister would come too and flirt with Tommy Lee or Guthrie. She had each of them as a boyfriend at one time or another. Lum wished Al had a sister closer to her age. But then, when she was with other girls, they didn't seem to like her or like the same things. She liked to climb trees when nobody was looking, but all the other girls just liked to sit under trees. She liked books and wished she had more. Sometimes she'd see girls trading books, but never with her. She could run fast, but no one would race her. The girls didn't race, and the boys scoffed when she challenged them to a race because she was a girl.

When Lum could get away from her chores, she'd play with the boys if she could sneak away from Granny. Once when she was ten, she and Walter and Al were going through the woods where their father cut firewood. They came upon the stump and the ax was sticking up from the wood.

"We was helping Daddy chop wood," Walter bragged.

"No you wasn't," Al said.

"Sure was. I was getting firewood ready for winter."

Lum said, "Daddy said you dragged the wood over to him and he used the ax."

"Lum! You don't know nothing. Where were you? Huh?"

She had been in the house, of course, so she didn't say anything.

"I help my daddy, too," Al said.

"Bet you don't chop no wood."

"Bet I chop as much as you do."

Lum thought, *That's right, each did as much as the other. None.*

"How do you do it?" she asked.

"Look here and I'll show you." Walter picked up a large branch. "First you chop it into pieces."

Two Pint appeared in the clearing. "What you doin'?"

"Go 'way," Walter said.

"I don't wanna go away."

"Come here, then."

Two Pint ran toward him. "Now kneel down by this stump." When he did as he was told, Walter said, "Lay your head down here."

"No!" Two Pint said.

"You chicken?" Walter taunted.

Lum stared. "What are you doing?"

"Just playing." Walter picked up the ax. "Two Pint, you want to know what a chicken feels right before its head gets chopped off?"

"I don't wanna," Two Pint whined.

So far Lum hadn't had to kill a chicken, although she'd seen it done many times. At first the chicken didn't even know it was dead.

"Al, hold him down."

Al squatted and put his hands on Two Pint's shoulders. Surely Walter wasn't going to hurt his brother, but Lum couldn't say anything. They wouldn't listen to her, and if she made a fuss they wouldn't let her play with them any more.

Walter lifted the ax and moved toward Two Pint, who started crying.

Al said, "Walter?"

"Don't worry, I'm just going to rest the ax on his neck so he knows what it's like to be a chicken." He had an odd grin as he said, "You want to play with us you can't act like a little boy."

She watched, transfixed, as Walter held the ax with both hands.

Sweat was on Al's face, and Two Pint's little body shook with silent sobs. Walter slowly lowered the blade towards Two Pint's neck. Al suddenly called out, "Walter, no! That ax might slip out of your hand."

Walter looked at his friend, lifted the ax, then backed away. "Get up, Two Pint. I guess you proved you're big enough to play with us."

But Lum no longer wanted to play with them. Not because of what they were about to do, but because she didn't have the nerve to stop it herself. Al did.

The Fuse Shortens

1933

"I'll miss you like a bear yearning for honey, but I'm going away," the Fat Lady wailed.

"Oh, we'll miss you, too," Daisy cried.

Violet asked, "Why you hafta go?"

"I been sold to the Russian circus. I'm taking the train to Pittsburgh." She held out her arms wide enough to encompass the twins. Lum pushed the cards together.

"Waaaahhhhh!" Meg wailed through the walls.

Even though the pictures showed Daisy and Violet joined at an angle, Lum imagined them curved in the Fat Lady's arms. The Fat Lady was parting from her friends, but Lum knew she'd befriend the Bearded Woman in the next sideshow. She looked forward to that part of the story.

"Shut that baby up!" Al's voice penetrated Lum's sanctuary.

"She'll hush after I rock her a while," Margaret said.

"You been rocking her. Check her diaper."

"Don't you think I already done that?"

"I'm tired of your lip, woman."

Heavy boots stomped outside Lum's room across the porch, and she heard the truck engine roar.

"Mercy," Lum whispered to herself. The Fat Lady went into her tent to pack up. She would never know how the Strongest Man on Earth felt about her. Meg's cries grew louder. Lighter footsteps headed toward Lum's little room. Lum gathered the postcards and

69

stuck them into her valise and snapped it shut just as Margaret pulled at the door.

"Lum, can me and Meg come in?"

"Of course." *Thank goodness for the hook holding the door closed,* she thought before opening it for the mother and squalling baby. Meg's head was redder than strawberry preserves.

"I can't do nothing with her," Margaret whined, holding Meg at arm's length.

"There, there," Lum cooed when she took the baby from Margaret. "Did you try some tonic for her teething?"

"Yes, and she's dry and I fed her a little while ago."

"Did you burp her?" Lum rubbed the small back, feeling the bumpy spine.

"Yeah."

"She don't feel hot, so I don't think she's ailing." She whispered, "Meggy Meg, it's all right, my little girl. My sweet girl." Over Meg's head she said, "Sometime babies just gotta cry. It's not easy being a baby, trying to get used to the world and big people talking loud, making noise. Babies know when things ain't right."

Margaret sank onto the bed. "Lum, Al's so upset about them wanting our place."

"I know. Maybe Meg's upset too. This is the onliest place she knows."

"Oh, that's silly." Margaret giggled.

One of Lum's tactics was to bring a little humor into a situation. But babies did know when people were angry or anxious.

"Did you check for a rash on her bottom?"

"Didn't see any last time I changed her."

"Bet it's colic. Sometimes when the mama's upset it carries through her milk and upsets the baby's tummy." Lum felt Meg's stomach. "Got any paregoric?"

"No. Last time I went to buy some, Mr. Reeves fussed at me so."

That rascal, Lum thought. *Al drank it all himself.* "We could make some catnip tea if you have any."

Margaret shook her head.

Lum looked at the ceiling. "Or I could go see Amy Read tomorrow to see if she has anything for colicky babies." And find out about Smiley.

"Oh, you don't need to go all the way over there. Mr. Reeves likes you. Bet he'll give you some paregoric. Works like this!" Margaret snapped her fingers. "All that tea and such takes such a long time."

"I'll try." Lum tried to hide her disappointment. She wanted to find out what was wrong with Smiley and felt guilty that she hadn't worried about him before seeing his empty house.

"How we gonna get through the night? If Al comes back and she's still a-crying, I don't know what'll happen."

"For now let's give her some more tonic. At least it'll calm her down. Not too much or she won't be able to sleep without it."

"Meg-Meg, you stay here with Auntie Lum, and I'm gonna fix you right up, little one," Margaret said.

A long scream came out of Meg's mouth, as if from an anguished soul.

"Mercy me," Lum said. "You got the strongest voice I ever heard. Yes, you do. You're waking all the dead in Stoneham County, yes, you are."

Margaret returned with the tonic and inserted an eyedropper full of dark syrup into the baby's mouth. Lum rubbed Meg's throat so she'd be sure to swallow. The screaming continued for a while, turned into sobs, then little whimpers, until she exhausted herself.

"Lum, I wish you could find out something for me." Margaret's voice shook.

"What's that?" Lum brushed her lips over the baby's soft hair.

"Could you find out who Al's girlfriend is?"

"Girlfriend? You think he has one?"

"He's got to, the way he's been acting lately. He didn't use to talk to me that way." She lowered her voice to a whisper. "He don't love me like he did. When we was first married he couldn't wait to get in bed with me. Now he acts like he dreads bedtime."

"I've been around enough married people to know that's what happens. You get used to each other. Doesn't mean he quit loving you."

"But you don't know how he used to look at me. Before Meg was born." Margaret traced a circle on the quilt. "When you go into town tomorrow, just keep your ears open, see if you can find out anything about Al."

"Margaret, I can't go around asking folks if they know if Al is stepping out on you. Nobody would say. They know I'm staying here."

"Everybody knows you keep secrets. People tell you things. Don't pretend they don't."

Lum sighed. "If I start asking, it'll get back to Al and he'll be mad at me."

"Cousin Lummy, it's you and me that's kin." She reached for Lum's wrist. "Remember when we was together all the time?"

True, Lum thought. *I always took care of Margaret. But this is too much.* "Of course I do. I've always loved you best. But I've also known Al all my life, he's almost like a brother."

"Blood's thicker than anything, ain't it?" She looked up at her. Lum had seen that look before when Margaret wanted something. She was hard to resist.

"I'll keep my ears open. Don't know if I'll hear anything." Her postcard people were easier to direct. No sticky situations or hard decisions.

"Whatever you find out—promise you'll tell me?"

"Yes." Lum didn't want to discover anything she'd have to repeat.

Little Margaret

1917

Little children always appealed to Lum more than those her own age. When her cousin June had little Margaret, Lum was sent over to stay with her a few weeks. Fresh out of her seventh year at school, she was glad to not have to work around the house. Her brothers would be planting and hoeing and weeding all through the long summer days until the lightning bugs let them know it was time for supper. June's ankles had swollen something awful before the baby was born, and the swelling hadn't gone down completely after she had given birth. The father, Rex, was disappointed that he didn't have a son and had little interest in his baby girl. So Lum coddled Margaret like she had her stuffed bunny and carried her around as she straightened up the house, took food to June's bed, and washed load after load of laundry. She wrestled the heavy denim overalls through the wringer. At home they only had a washboard, so she wasn't used to the big machine.

Each summer, Lum moved to June's house. There was a new baby each year, including a scrawny boy after three girls. Margaret was special, though, Lum's first baby. When Lum graduated from high school, she stayed on after summer and no one asked her back home.

Margaret was four then. She told Lum, "I'm big now and Mama wanth me to help with Robbie."

"You are? That's an important job, taking care of babies," Lum said. If she'd been the oldest in her family, things would have been different.

Margaret said, "I don't like babies."

"You don't? But babies are so sweet."

73

Margaret shook her head, red curls bouncing. "They cry all the time and poop their diapers and they can't tell you wuth wrong. It's not fair! I wish I wasn't the big girl."

"Your mama needs help. Four babies . . ."

"Four?" Margaret ticked off her little fingers. "Elsie is three, and Bertha is two, so Robbie is the only baby."

As far as Rex is concerned, Robbie is the only child, Lum thought.

"You listen to your mama. Soon Robbie won't be a baby anymore."

"There's always another baby." Margaret grabbed Lum's hand. "Let's go to the creek."

She let the little girl lead her down the narrow path to Crooked Creek. "Cousin Lummy, do you like babies more than you like me?"

"More than you?" Lum picked up her little cousin and held her close. "I don't like nobody better'n you. You're my little baby always. Even when you're grown, I'll like you best, 'cause you're my first little baby." She stroked Margaret's hair.

"And I like you the beth because you'll always be my Lummy." Her little arms squeezed Lum as she wrapped her legs around Lum's waist. "Carry me to the creek."

"You're getting heavy, Margaret." Lum had her arms under Margaret's bottom. "Why don't you ride on my back?"

"Like a hobby horth?"

"Yeah, like your hobby horse." She moved Margaret to her back.

"Giddy up, Horthy," Margaret said, digging her heels into Lum's back.

Lum galloped to Crooked Creek with Margaret giggling into her neck. Lum often came there by herself. She had discovered a little beach area where she would take off her shoes and stockings and wade to a log where she'd sit with toes wide apart, letting the stream flow between, tickling them. She'd listen to the water gurgle over flat rocks like Jimmy would guzzle water after working all day, his throat going gulp, gulp, gulp. Sometimes she'd see a leaf being pushed downstream. It would get caught between two rocks, but the water would be insistent on that leaf moving and the force of it would push, cajole, and torment the leaf until it left its place of safety to continue its journey. This was the first time she'd ever brought anyone else here. Would it be ruined now by bringing Margaret? She wouldn't take Margaret to the log, she'd keep her on the beach. She sat by the creek with her legs crossed and put Margaret on her lap.

"See that leaf?" Lum pointed to a crisp yellow oak leaf that was being tumbled by the current.

"Where?"

"That yellow one. See how it's being pushed by the water?"

Margaret looked around until she saw the leaf Lum had pointed out. "I see it!"

"Think it'll make it past those rocks?"

"Yes. Go, leaf, go." She sprang off Lum's lap. "I'll help it," she said, running toward the creek.

"No! Stop!" Lum ran after her. "It's slippery right there," she called after the child, who ran so fast Lum couldn't overtake her before she reached the creek.

Margaret jumped in with both feet, splashing. She disappeared for a moment, then she bobbed up and tried to stand, but the current knocked her down. Lum hurried into the creek still wearing her shoes and grabbed Margaret around the waist and lifted her up. Margaret wailed.

"Did you hurt yourself?"

But Margaret kept sobbing, and buried her face in Lum's neck. Her dress was soaked and water seeped into Lum's full-length apron. Fortunately she hadn't hit her head; her red hair was dry. It was cool out, and Lum hoped the water wouldn't give Margaret a cold.

"Let's get you home and dried off." As she carried Margaret back, Lum's feet squishing, she didn't care how heavy the child was, she just needed to take good care of her. And keep her safe.

Lum Asks Questions

1933

The bright sun warmed Lum's face, but her aching feet predicted rain before the day would be over. She trod through a thick layer of sycamore leaves toward the small log cabin where Amy Read lived.

She'd heard about Amy, the midwife, long before she met her. Amy had delivered Lum and all her brothers. She'd been fishing when Two Pint was born, so Lum had never seen Amy come to the house to help her mother. When they got back from fishing, Granny was holding Two Pint and no one was allowed in Mama's room. They only saw the bloody sheet being carried out by the tall, light brown woman, her head bent.

Sixteen years later, when Ethel had Junior, Amy came to the house. Since it was a long delivery, Amy spent some of the time sitting on the porch smoking a pipe. Lum hadn't wanted to hear Ethel's screams, so she'd rocked alongside Amy. Lum wanted to ask Amy about her past as a slave, but was hesitant. She didn't know any other colored people who had been slaves, so she wondered if being a slave was much different than working in the tobacco fields for Cyrus Snell. Amy and Smiley were about the only coloreds who didn't work on Snell lands.

She struggled to think of something to say and then the midwife said, "You was the most special baby I ever birthed. I just knew you'd grow up to be one powerful woman."

Lum approached the cabin feeling both powerful and weak, most of the time more weak than powerful. Her body was powerful, but she often felt weak-willed around other people. But the eighty-something-year-old woman who answered the door was powerful in will as her once-powerful body aged.

"Miz Lum," Amy said. "Are you ailing?"

"No, it's Meg. She's colicky."

"Come on in and I'll fix up some catnip for you." She opened the oak door wide enough for Lum to spy Smiley before she stepped inside.

He sat up in a bed in the far corner, his heavily bandaged knee resting on a pile of quilts.

"Smiley! What?"

He grimaced. "Hadn't you heard?"

"Al told me about you being by the side of the road. Mr. Snell . . ."

"That's who done it to me. That ol'. . . Well, I better not say."

"But why'd he do it?"

"He hates me. For who I am. For being my mother's child. For having my own business. For carrying furniture he thinks I ain't got no right to have."

"What?" Lum sank into a chair by the bed.

"It's a long story, but Mr. Harper and me had a plan to sell some of my furniture at an auction. Turns out the auction was for Mrs. Snell's family, 'cause her daddy died. I was in my wagon carrying my furniture and Snell stopped me and whacked me with a cane. One of my own canes." He gestured to his knee. "So I got me a busted up knee and Miz Amy's taking care of me. I was passed out for weeks."

"You were knocked out by my medicine," Amy said. "That wild lettuce'll keep a body asleep, sure will." She reached into a large sack and pulled out a handful of dried herbs. She spread it out on her pine table. Turning to Lum, she said, "Wanted to keep him still as could be so that knee'll set right." She added a couple of pinches of an herb to the other. "Now you boil this down and give her a little bit whenever you hear her fussing."

Maybe some of the wild lettuce would give Margaret a good night's sleep, either taken by herself or by Meg. "Is it wild lettuce?"

Amy chuckled. "Lord's sake, no. A little chamomile to help her sleep." She shook her head, chuckling. "Wild lettuce for a baby, my my."

"Well, thank you. How much?"

"Just a penny."

Smiley called out. "Oh, Miz Lum, I sold them men's cuff links for you. Got ten dollars for 'em. Money's back at my house, but I'll pay you when I can."

Ten dollars. She felt relief mixed with guilt. But they were hers to sell, even if they had belonged to her great granddaddy.

A light wind accompanied Lum across the town square. Snow geese gathered around the pond, and a fat pigeon was perched on Lord Fairfax's granite head. Maybe she'd be able to get some bread crumbs for the birds later—if they weren't already gone to Florida or further south. Signs were posted on the outer edges of the square: "County Meeting. Scenic Parkway Plans. First Baptist Church. All Land Owners Welcome. 6:00 Tonight."

When Lum approached the pharmacy, she wondered if she dared ask for more paregoric. The worst that could happen is Mr. Reeves would say "No." Wouldn't hurt to ask. Amy wouldn't give wild lettuce to a baby, but it sounded like it worked like paregoric. She pushed open the heavy door and headed for the back. "Good morning, Mr. Reeves."

"Lum, what a pleasant surprise." He looked out the window—for Al's truck, Lum assumed. "How are you doing?"

Mr. Reeves was a newcomer to Granite Falls. He'd only lived there ten or twelve years, so maybe he didn't know anything about her except that she took care of different folks.

"I'm helping out at Mr. Shay's during the day now. He's under the weather, you know."

"Miss Liza brought in a prescription a couple days ago. Is it helping?"

"He's still coughing something awful. Spitting up blood."

He shook his head. "Not much we can do for pneumonia."

"I reckon not. He's getting lots of sleep, so maybe the medicine's helping him that way."

"Is he needing a refill?"

"I'm not here for Mr. Shay. I was wondering what we could do about a colicky baby." Lum rubbed her ear. "I think Baby Meg busted my eardrum last night."

"When I was in the war, they'd have these sirens before the bombs landed. I swear, when my Roger was little, he was louder than those sirens."

"Don't seem like their little bodies could make so much noise, does it?" She rested her elbows on the high counter. As usual, it hadn't a speck of dust.

"No, it sure don't. You needing something for your eardrums or for Meg?"

She chuckled. "Meg."

"Now, look here, Lum, it wasn't that long ago you came in here wanting paregoric for her. She done took all that already?"

"I reckon so. Margaret said they were all out."

Mr. Reeves looked Lum up and down. She felt his gaze rest on her bosom, then move up her neck. "That baby took all that paregoric, she'd be sleeping 'round the clock. I told you to keep it away from Al. I'll sell you one more bottle." He leaned closer and Lum could tell he'd had onions for lunch. "I don't want to see you, Margaret, Al, none of his friends, or Baby Meg herself in here asking for more before Christmas. Am I clear?"

Lum swallowed. "Yes, sir. I'm gonna keep this bottle hid. Nobody but me will know where it is."

"Don't disappoint me." He turned away to retrieve the medicine.

"Just wondering." Lum paused. "Has Al been back in here?"

"Oh, he knows better than to try getting anything out of me." He batted his hand dismissively. "He sends his friends to pick up stuff for him."

How could she ask if he'd ever seen Al with a woman without just coming out and asking? She couldn't be so obvious.

"What friends?"

"That Guinea been working for him came here last week. I'm not selling those people no drugs." He shook his finger. "Not without a prescription, and they won't go to the doctor."

"For some folks it's hard to pay a doctor and for drugs."

Scowling, Mr. Reeves handed her a small sack. "I'm just following the laws. I'm not losing my license over this. For infant use only."

She wanted to ask what other friends, were any of them women, but she didn't want to leave with Mr. Reeves mad at her, so she tried to think of how to get back in his good graces.

"I'll bet you and the Mrs. are enjoying Roger's little ones."

"They're just the brightest little scamps you ever did see." He beamed. "Me and Roger took the boy over to the quarry last Saturday to watch the big trucks. He sure liked that."

"And the girl?"

"She's helping Ruth Ann cut out scraps for quilts. Grandchildren are a joy."

"You ever need any help with 'em, let me know."

"Don't reckon we will, but we'll keep you in mind." He was looking out the window again.

Lum turned to go, then stopped. "What's this meeting about tonight?"

"The Scenic Road. I think they're gonna try to convince the farmers to sell their land."

Lum could feel her heartbeat speed up. "What if they don't want to sell?"

"Be foolish not to. That road's going through one way or 'nother. Best thing that could happen to us." His words tumbled out faster. "It's gonna bring lots of folks through here. I'm gonna put in a soda fountain and a lunch counter." He waved toward a corner of the pharmacy where a couple of chairs sat.

"My goodness! Well, I best be getting over to the Shays' house. Bye, Mr. Reeves."

"Take care of yourself, Lum. Remember, for infant use only."

For a peaceful night, she thought, slipping the bag between her breasts. *What did that mean "one way or another"? Will Al be forced to sell or else? Or else what? Have those road people talked to Walter and Jimmy too? Will my family farm have to be sold?*

Lum knew the story of the farm as all farm children did. Her father had told about Jedidiah Carson, who fought in the Revolutionary War and was given land in the frontier, as western Virginia was called at the time. His family packed up all the belongings they could carry in a wagon with seven children and made their way from the Virginia coast down the James River. They disembarked at Columbia and stayed in the little town long enough for Elizabeth, Jedidiah's wife, to give birth to a baby they named Columbia. They continued on through Indians, bears, and other terrors. The land was rocky and hilly, but they found enough flat land to plant a garden to sustain a large family that soon grew through marriage and grandchildren. Each son was given part of the land when he married. Each generation had at least one person who kept careful records of births, deaths, and marriages. The names Jedidiah and Columbia cropped up every couple of generations. By the time Lum's father inherited the land, each farm was only an acre or two at the most, some even smaller. Two Pint, Guthrie, and Tommy Lee were gone, and Jimmy and Walter decided that rather than divide an already small farm in half, they would run the farm together. Walter hadn't married, so he was content to stay in the old house with Jimmy and Ethel. But Walter, as the younger, unmarried, brother, was hardly considered an equal. Everyone considered it Jimmy's land, and he was certainly the boss. Even Ethel, who came from a larger farm, felt that it was hers and Jimmy's. To her, Walter was just the errant brother. And Lum was the helpful sister, not considered part of the farm.

Frozen
1918

O nce Jimmy had married Ethel, giving Granny another woman to help out, nothing stood in the way of Lum living year-round with Cousin June and her children. Until, one February day, Two Pint showed up.

"Hey, Lum, you gotta come home. It's Granny."

She turned her head from where she'd been resting her cheek on the warm milk cow's side. "Granny? What's wrong?" She continued squeezing, hearing the milk join the bucket.

"You're needed at home. Bring your clothes."

"Let me take the milk in the kitchen." *Why does Granny want me back home?* she wondered.

"June there?"

She nodded, lifting the bucket.

"Want me to help carry it?"

"If you don't mind." She could carry it herself, but if he was willing to wait while she put together her things, at least she'd have company on the walk back. "Granny sick?"

"I'll tell you and June together so I don't have to say it twice."

In the kitchen, June was scrambling eggs. "Two Pint!" she squealed. "What you doing here so early?"

"It's Granny."

"What happened?"

So something did happen to Granny. "What?" she echoed.

"Sometime during the night, we don't know what happened, but she froze up. One side of her."

"Froze up? What do you mean?"

Two Pint touched his cheek with his fingertips. He had a bad case of acne, making him look like he'd been stung all over his face. "She can't talk or lift her right arm. Walter went to get the doctor, and I come to get Lum."

"Oh my," June said. "Anything I can do?"

"I don't rightly know. Just wanted to tell you about Granny. Maybe you could tell other people in the family."

"I will. Oh, damn! I burnt them eggs." She pushed her fork under the yellow mass. "I can fix most of it."

"What you mean, Granny can't talk?" Lum asked as her brother accompanied her to her room to pack up her clothes in a flour sack. She was glad her three cards—the Snake Woman, one of the Siamese twins, and one of a woman without arms—were beneath her clothes.

"She opens her mouth and makes a little noise, but she can't push no words out."

She couldn't imagine Granny without words. They had talked a lot, more to each other than to anyone else in the family. When her brothers and Daddy came in from working they either took over the conversation or were so hungry they ate without talking. Lum flung her clothes into the sack without folding. Granny needed her, she had to hurry. Two Pint was rubbing his face and she could almost hear Granny saying, "Don't pick at your pimples, you'll make it worse." But Granny couldn't talk. Doctor Miles would be there soon. Lum wondered if Granny had been to the doctor after he'd examined Lum years earlier. It sounded like Granny didn't think much of him and now he was the only person who could help her.

Walking from June's farm to her own, Lum could hardly keep from running on the frosty ground. She had to see Granny. Maybe she'd be all right by now. When they reached the gate, she noticed a black horse with leather saddlebags that she didn't recognize. It must be the doctor's. She sped into the house and up the stairs. Granny's door was closed and Ethel paced the hall.

"Glad you could come back. She's bad off."

Lum tried the door handle.

"Dr. Miles is examining her." Ethel crossed her arms.

Examining? Lum imagined the doctor doing to Granny what he'd done to her when she'd been poked and prodded all over.

"When I got to the kitchen this morning, she weren't there. You know she can't stay in bed when there's even a little glimmer of light."

Lum nodded. Ethel had replaced her.

"So I come upstairs and there she laid, making this noise like deep in her throat, and when I started asking questions it was clear she can't say a word. I said, 'Can I help you get up?' but she shook her head and I saw her arm hanging off the side of the bed like a shirt sleeve on a clothes line. She reached over with her other arm and put it up on the bed and I realized something bad happened. Walter was the first one to breakfast and I told him lickety split to go fetch the doctor and when Two Pint come in I sent him after you." She stopped to take a breath. "Dr. Miles just got here. Your daddy told all the boys to get to work, wasn't nothing they could do, so they're all outside. Except I left some biscuits and gravy for Walter and Two Pint. Can you go fix 'em something else?"

"I want to see Granny."

"There ain't nothing to do for her until the doctor's through."

Lum didn't want to go downstairs. She should be right there when the doctor came out. But Ethel had taken over. "Ethel, would you come get me as soon as the doctor is finished? I want to hear firsthand what he has to say."

Ethel narrowed her eyes at Lum. "You don't trust me to tell you what he says?"

"No, it's not that . . . I just want to be able to ask questions if I have any."

"I'll let you in on it, but don't you think your daddy wants to hear, too? He's her son."

"You're right. Should I go get him?"

"After you fix them boys some decent breakfast."

It didn't matter anyway, because when Dr. Miles came out of Granny's room he would only talk to Lum's father. He wouldn't say a word until Lum brought her father back from the field. All the boys followed and Lum went in to see Granny while the doctor was with her father.

She whispered, "Granny."

The old woman's head raised a little and she made a half-smile.

Everything on the right side of her face drooped—her eye, her cheek, her mouth. Lum took her right arm, but it felt limp, like the dead snake Jimmy had thrown at Lum one time. For a long time afterward she had felt the phantom floppy weight of the carcass. Lum squeezed her grandmother's hand, but it stayed still—the hand with strong purple veins, the hand that showed her how to make a pie crust, the hand that held hers when she went to the doctor. But she couldn't let go. She knew she should have lifted the one that still was alive, unfrozen. The right hand didn't work, but it was still a part of her grandmother. "Granny, I love you." She didn't know if she had ever told her grandmother that before. Her family didn't talk about love, just duty and responsibility. And family.

With her good hand, Granny pointed to her heart and then Lum's. She motioned with her left hand the act of writing.

"You want a pen and paper?" Lum asked.

Granny nodded.

Lum didn't want to leave, didn't want to put down the hand, but she kissed the big knuckles of thin fingers and placed the hand on the quilt. She closed one eye so she would only see the left side of her grandmother's face. The true half.

When she went back into the hall, the doctor was gone. Her daddy told them, "She had a stroke, there wasn't nothing Dr. Miles could do for her. He said keep her still and make sure she stays flat on her back. After a few days, maybe she'll improve, maybe she won't. Sometimes folks who have strokes never get better, but some do. She may never talk again even if the feeling comes back into her extremities, well, her arm and leg."

Lum stayed home and cared for Granny. Knowing how much Granny disdained the doctor, Lum ignored his advice. Once a day, propping her up, she let the old woman write with her left hand. The handwriting was almost as undecipherable as her speech, but once Lum learned how to decipher, she and Granny could talk. The only thing Granny had believed the doctor about was that Lum should forget about getting married. Mostly Granny told her to be a good girl and take care of her family.

Landowners Meeting

1933

Leaves were drifting down, gently rustling as they brushed against branches and finally settled on the ground at dusk. Liza had given Lum a dollar bill for another day of feeding Dan, then sitting while he slept. She had put it inside her dress beside the paper sacks with Amy's herbs and the paregoric. The bags mimicked the sound of leaves as she walked across the town square. Men were sitting outside the general store eating sandwiches. A few yards away from them sat Kenny in his brown uniform.

"Hello, Miss Lum," he called out.

Approaching warily, she replied, "Hello, there. Work over for the day?"

"Yep, we got off a little early so as we can go to the meetin'."

Lum motioned toward the men, all wearing brown pants and shirts. "They your crew?"

"Used to be. They don't like me none. My job's gonna change soon."

"Is that good?"

Kenny shrugged. "Have to see. This new man wants me to talk to the folks up on the Knob about moving out of their houses and going to some new town. Might get myself shot."

"Shot?"

"My people don't like outsiders telling them what to do. I'm almost a outsider my own self since I been gone so long. But Mr. Shapiro, he says they'll listen to me 'cause I'll tell 'em how it'll be better if they take some money and go somewhere else." He looked at her. "Not sure I believe him, but he offered me good money."

His steely, blue-gray eyes were hard to look away from. "Lady in the store don't like me neither. She wouldn't cut none of that hoop cheese for me. Usually she wants to trade for some sang, but she said the Sang Man done come and gone and she ain't fooling with none of us 'til next fall when we gather more sang for him."

"Heaven's sakes, I'll get you a sandwich." She pulled her eyes away. "Stay right here."

"Don't have to do that," he mumbled, but pulled a dime out of his pocket and handed it to her. "And a Co'cola?"

As much as she hated having to pass the throng of men by the store, she hated more that none of them bothered to get him a sandwich. Sure his kind was different, but they had to eat, didn't they? She also hated having to see that sour Miss Bridges again. After buying a chunk of wheel cheese, bread, and a Coca Cola, it was all Lum could do not to ask, "His money's not good enough for you, but from my hand it's fine?" But she silently paid and returned to the grassy area.

"Here, Kenny." She handed him the food.

"You staying for the meeting? It's gonna be about the road."

"I would like to find out where this road's a-going." Her feet hurt, so if she stayed for the meeting, at least she wouldn't have to walk back up the mountain right away.

Kenny wiped his mouth with a dingy handkerchief. "They asked us workers to stay. Course we can't say nothing, that's for the landowners. But Mr. Snell thought it'd be good if people get to know what we look like."

"Mr. Snell's involved in this?"

"He called the meeting." He tipped the glass bottle skyward, draining it. "Him and Mr. Shapiro, the man who talked to me today." A loud cola burp erupted. He covered his mouth, looking sheepish.

"One time this revenue man came to our house and was talking to Papa. I was a young'un so I didn't know nothing about what they was talking about, but all of a sudden, he called out to Early, 'Get me my gun. Not the squirrel gun, the man-shooting gun!' We laughed watching that man run on down the road. Din't never see him around the Knob again." He chuckled. "After that all one of us had to say was 'get me my man-shooting gun,' and we'd bust out laughing."

Lum thought, *He wouldn't think it was so funny if, as he said, someone on the Knob tried to shoot him.* But she wouldn't bring that back up.

Farmers were starting to gather around the entrance to the Baptist
Church at the eastern edge of the square. Lum saw Al in the middle
of a group of noisy men, her brother Walter with them, gesturing
wildly. *Oh, please don't let them act up in public.* She couldn't count the
number of times Al and Walter had gotten into trouble together, egging
each other on.

The white steeple seemed to puncture clouds that were getting
grayer by the minute. When Kenny finished eating, he and Lum
ambled toward the church, folks in the crowd glaring as Kenny passed.
Cyrus Snell and his son, Braxton, were standing on either side of the
open church doors like deacons for Sunday services. Al and Walter had
already entered. She bet their group was not going to just sit quietly.
A man in a suit too warm for the weather motioned Kenny over. Lum
continued alone, eyes down. She aimed for the elder Snell's side, but
Braxton blocked the doorway when he saw her, saying, "Landowners
only," then greeted the man behind her. She felt her cheeks burn. *Who
did he think he was to turn me away?* Standing on the top step of the
church, she looked for someone to enter with. Jimmy and Ethel were in
the back of the crowd. Jimmy's Sunday fedora shaded his face. She wove
her way through the people ascending the steps.

"Jimmy, can I sit with y'all?"

"You don't own a farm."

"It's our family's farm," Lum said. "Not just yours and Walter's."

"Don't start that again, Lum. Just come on and don't say nothing.
Ethel wouldn't stay behind neither."

"It concerns me, too." Ethel spat out the words. She was wearing
a blue and pink flowered dress and gray sweater, its hemline a little
uneven.

When they reached the entrance again, Cyrus Snell clapped Jimmy
on the back in welcome, shaking his hand with the other.

"They're with me," Jimmy said, indicating Ethel and Lum.

Snell bent his neck slightly. "You folks go on up to the front."

Ethel nudged Lum with her elbow. "Never seen him so chummy,"
she whispered.

Farmers were directed to the middle front section of pews, road workers occupied the back rows. Jimmy led his wife and sister to the fourth row. Lum could see Al's scalp, a small circle at the crown of his head, and Walter's curly dark hair beneath his cap, in the front row. Leaning across Ethel, Lum asked Jimmy, "Anybody come to you about selling the farm?"

"Damn fools talked to Walter, not me. He can't make no decision 'cause we both own it. I got to find out what the whole story is, not just what Walter says. You know how he mixes things up."

"But what did they say?"

"Something about some of our land in the way. Not all of it."

"So they want to buy a portion."

"I don't know! I gotta learn more about it, that's why I'm here. Now don't keep talking."

Lum leaned back and looked around the sanctuary. A few farm wives were there, but the crowd was mostly men. Town business owners—the owner of the feed mill, the barber, Mr. Reeves, Miss Bridges, Doctor Meadows, and the owner of the sawmill—all sat on the left side first two row of seats. On the right side were several men Lum had never seen before—a few wearing suits, most in brown uniforms—and Kenny. She didn't see any of Kenny's people. Although the Melungeons owned land, unless they had come into town, they wouldn't have known about the meeting. The road men must really be relying on Kenny to tell his kind about what was going on. Some of the town people sat on the sides; no sign of Liza Shay or other single professional women, such as the librarian or the postmistress. Cyrus and Braxton Snell sat near the altar looking pleased with themselves. As church deacons, they were in their usual Sunday positions.

"Welcome, neighbors," the Baptist minister said. "The First Baptist Church of Granite Falls is happy to host this meeting of the citizens of Stoneham County. Let's begin with a prayer to our Lord Jesus Christ."

After the prayer, the minister looked at the road workers first, scanned the crowd, and said, "I look forward to seeing all of you in church on Sunday. We have Sunday School at eight and services at nine and eleven. Join us for fellowship after each service. Now, Mr. Cyrus Snell is going to introduce our speaker today."

Mr. Snell clasped his hands in front of his belt buckle. ' ning. I'm happy so many of you have come out to hear abou dawning for Stoneham County and Granite Falls. We may but Granite Falls will soon be well-known, as folks from a the United States will be traveling through here as they drive on the new scenic highway. Please join me in welcoming Mr. Shapiro from the Resettlement Administration."

Lum recognized the man who had looked at the view from Al and Margaret's farm in late summer. In a heavy suit, his appearance was as jarring as his heavy Brooklyn accent when he addressed the crowd: "The Roosevelt administration has decided to continue the fine Skyline Drive because this is the most beautiful countryside in our great nation. Right where you live. Isn't that true?"

A smattering of applause came from the business owners.

"President Roosevelt knows well the hardships of this age. He is on your side. He wants every citizen of the United States to have a good-paying job all year long, no matter if crops fail or weather goes bad. Just ask any of the workmen. Some'a them are your sons, your brothers, your grandsons. Others have left their homes to take advantage of the opportunity to build a fine roadway through the mountains." With a stubby hand, he indicated the road workers in the back. "If you asked them, to a man, they'd tell you they're happy to have this work. The Civilian Conservation Corps will be working here, too, creating a park alongside the road. That's why we're calling it the Blue Ridge Parkway."

Lum leaned forward, trying to catch every word out of his thick accent.

"But this scenic road is not just going to help the young men from farms. It's gonna bring prosperity to your area. The Blue Ridge Parkway will go from Virginia all the way to the southern part of North Carolina and even into Tennessee." He spread his arms wide, gold cufflinks glistening.

It's all my fault, Lum thought. *I had to go and tell Mr. Shapiro that Al's view was the best around. No wonder they want his land.*

Mr. Shapiro continued, "The idear is for travelers to enjoy the beautiful scenery as they motor through. Now, by making a parkway, there will be a lot of land alongside the road. President Roosevelt wants tourists to enjoy rocky vistas as well as pasture land."

"Folks want to look at cows?" one of the farmers exclaimed.

Mr. Snell said, "We'll have plenty of time for questions later. Let Mr. Shapiro finish."

"The Civilian Conservation Corps will be enhancing the natural beauty of your area alongside the scenic highway. If your land is where the road's going, you probably already have had a visit from me or Mr. Walsh. But we haven't spoken to everyone yet. Mr. Kenneth Doyle . . ." Kenny's head jerked up at the sound of his name. "Stand up, Kenny."

Kenny stood briefly, but quickly sat. *"Mr."?* Lum thought. *No one around here calls a Melungeon "Mr."*

"He'll be going with us to talk to the folks in his community about this opportunity."

Lum heard whispering: "Why'd they pick him, an ex-con?" "Just got out of prison." "I heard he done killed a man." "They'll get shot they go wandering up Hopkin's Knob by theirselves." Lum's neck felt stiff. Laying her cold hand on it eased the pain.

"President Roosevelt has created whole new towns just for people who are going to be relocated. These people will be able to build a new house for themselves and will be assured of a job in a factory. This program will lift folks out of a dead-end existence."

Lum wondered: What dead-end existence? Was her life at a dead end? She was good at helping with the young and the sick. Would working in a factory be better? She'd heard of places where women sit and sewed. She could sew, but why do it in a factory? Oh, it was too much to think about. Out of the corner of her eye, she saw wavy lines moving through the air. Like a current in the stream, they'd undulate down, then be replaced by new waves. She knew a bad headache was coming.

The crowd was muttering.

"You want to know how it affects *you*. So I'm calling back my new friend, Mr. Snell, to tell you how you can benefit from the scenic parkway."

"Hey, Cyrus, would you tell us what that Jew fella just said?" a voice called out.

"Say it in English!"

Braxton glared at the crowd.

Cyrus Snell held up a hand. "Mr. Shapiro is a government official. Show some respect. Mr. Walsh, from the Virginia State Highway Commission, has visited with some of you. I must say the government is making very generous offers. Wouldn't you say, Mr. Woodward?" He addressed a man sitting in the front row.

"Yes, sir," the elderly man agreed.

"Mr. Woodward has received a hefty payment for his entire farm, yet he will continue to live there in peace."

"He'll be dead time the road goes through," Ethel whispered to Lum. "What does he care? He ain't got no young'uns to leave his land to."

"And Mr. and Mrs. Hayes have agreed to sell their land for a pretty penny, let me tell you. Enough to buy a nice house on Jefferson Street. They never dreamed they'd be able to afford to live on Jefferson Street." Cyrus looked at the farmers.

"Then there's Mr. and Mrs. Bennett, who are going to move to Wigtown, one of the new cities. Mr. Bennett will be the general manager at the cotton mill. He'll be in a modern house with all the newest improvements—running water, an indoor bathroom, and electricity. So you can see, this is the best thing for you all." Cyrus Snell beamed at the crowd.

Al said, "Can we ask questions now?"

Be nice, Al. Don't make an enemy of the Snells, Lum thought.

"Why certainly, Mr. Lewis."

"I got lots of questions." Al scratched his head. "First, no disrespect, but Mr. Hayes and Mr. Woodward are old. What would a man of working age be able to do living in town when all he knows is farming? And how many general managers can one cotton mill have?"

Some laughter erupted at the second question.

"I'm glad you asked that, Mr. Lewis. These two gentlemen have worked hard all their lives and they deserve a nice home, don't they?" Cyrus made eye contact with some of the farmers. "Truth is, Mr. Woodward has agreed for his farm to go to the government upon his death." He looked around. "He already has a check deposited in the bank. The government is generously letting him stay in the house where he's lived all his life. Can't beat that, can you?"

"But—" Al said. Lum hoped he wouldn't make Snell angry but keep asking good questions. No telling what would happen between two men with such tempers.

"Let me answer your second question before you have a third or fourth. We want others to have a chance, too." This time Snell's look was harder. "Mr. Bennett was offered the job of general manager because of the number of workers he has supervised as one of my foremen while still raising his own tobacco crop. I hate to see him go. But," he held his palms out, "the government's offer was so grand, how could he say 'No'?"

"But what about younger farmers?" Al asked.

"Let's let someone else ask a question."

Walter, sitting next to Al, raised his hand. Snell looked away and pointed at a farmer sitting on Lum's row.

"Mr. Snell, some of us are wondering what you're getting out of this?"

Cyrus took a step backward, rubbed his thinning hair against his scalp, then answered, "I've agreed to sell some of my land up High Ford Road."

"He ain't growing nothing on it no ways," mumbled Jimmy.

"There's sharecroppers' cabins," Lum said. Darkening clouds looked purple against the pink sky.

"Won't hurt his feelings none to kick 'em out," Ethel said.

Snell next called on a large man with a straw hat. "What if the offer they make ain't as much as I paid for my land?"

"I doubt that'd happen." The two Snells exchanged glances.

Walter waved his hand.

"Mr. Carson." Snell nodded at Walter.

"Oh no," Jimmy muttered.

Lum's brother stood. "What I wanna know is this." He shook his finger at Cyrus, his voice rising. "What can a man do if all he knows is farming and he don't want to work in no factory and he don't want no damn house on no damned Jefferson Street?"

The crowd erupted, yelling. Lum wished they'd quiet down. Her head was starting to throb above her right eye.

"That's a good question, and every one of you wants to know the answer. If Mr. Shapiro or Mr. Walsh makes you an offer on your land, listen to him. The Highway Commission . . ." he turned to the two officials. "I hope I don't get in no trouble saying this. They got big bucks. You may just get enough dough to buy you a new farm somewhere else."

"But what if we don't want no other farm?" someone called out. "My land's been in the family since before the War Between the States. My wife's farm was given to her great-great-great-granddaddy for fighting right beside George Washington."

Lum heard others giving dates—1790, 1905, 1832—how long their land had been in their families.

"We didn't come as no carpetbaggers," someone called out.

Snell reddened.

"I ain't selling for no price!" Al yelled.

"You ain't gettin' mine!"

"Gentlemen," Snell boomed, "this is no way to act around these visitors."

"Better not visit me lessen they wanna look down the barrel of a shotgun."

Lum's cool hand cradled her forehead. What was this crowd about to do? She'd never seen people turn against Cyrus Snell like this.

Mr. Walsh stepped forward, hands held high, and drawled, "We want a better life for you mountain people."

"Mountain people?"

"We don't need your help!"

"Don't want no handouts!" Walter yelled.

"Shut up," Jimmy muttered. "I'm gonna bust his ass when we get home."

Cyrus stepped close to the front row near Al and Walter. "These gentlemen have taken time to explain the benefits of this parkway, and you've been rude. I'm ashamed of my county."

"*Your* county?!" The temperature seemed to rise when the farmers starting shouting.

Snell stepped back a few feet, his words drowned out by loud voices. Braxton joined his father in front of the pulpit, his face tight, and announced, "Meeting adjourned."

Al stood on the front pew, faced the crowd, and whistled a long, piercing sound. When the noise level lowered, he announced, "*Our meeting will continue at the roadhouse.*" As people rose, he added, "No rich men or government men allowed."

Lum sat quietly, her head throbbing, while everyone thronged out of the sanctuary. She didn't know what worried her more: Al raising a ruckus, or Margaret's fit when she'd have to tell her Al was going to the roadhouse. When the crowd carried its anger outside, she followed. People were milling about, some arguing loudly.

"Why're you here, Lum?" Walter called.

"It affects me, too." Lum crossed her arms over her breasts, hoping he didn't hear the crackle of the hidden paper sack. "Those men talk to you?"

Walter grimaced. "Yeah, Mr. Walsh. They want the front acreage along the road. Said we could move our house back. But we can't have no garden further back, it's too shady, and they say can't nobody cut the trees. Folks near Roanoke did, and they had to pay big fines for harvesting their own timber. How can they tell us what to do on our own land? See, they make all these rules so everybody'll just sell the whole place. But we ain't selling."

Al strode toward her. "Lum, does Margie know you're here?"

"I just found out about the meeting today, so I came over after leaving the Shays. I'll be getting on up there," she added.

"Tell her not to expect me for supper. I'll eat at the roadhouse. Coming, Jimmy?"

Jimmy shook his head. "Y'all go on. Come on, Lum, we'll carry you up to Al's."

Suddenly, Lum remembered Margaret with her colicky baby and hated herself for not hurrying up there with the paregoric and Amy's herbs. Margaret would probably fuss at her. A small spot of pain centered over her right eyebrow as if a single bullet had pierced her forehead.

"Hey, Al," Kenny called out.

Al spun around. "I reckon I know whose side you're on." He spat on the ground and strode toward a couple of farmers who waited for him while Kenny stood with his mouth open.

"He killed his own brother," Ethel said to Lum. "Life don't mean the same to them."

"It was his brother-in-*law*," Lum explained. "An accident. They didn't mean to kill him. But the man was running around on Kenny's sister. And she was expecting."

"Lum, prison is full of innocent men. Not a one of 'em committed the crime they's in for," Jimmy pronounced.

"He told me the whole story," Lum protested.

"I'd stay away from him I was you," Ethel said. "No telling what he'd do to ya if you're alone with him."

"I don't intend to spend any time with him."

"I seen you talking with him by the store," Ethel pointed out.

Lum pulled herself up to her full height and looked down at her sister-in-law. "I got to know him at Al and Margaret's. I don't think it's right the store is only too glad to take the sang those people dig up but they won't let 'em inside otherwise. That sound right to you?"

"Well!" Ethel replied, her lips tighter than a quilt stitch. Lum squeezed into Jimmy's pickup next to Ethel, half her buttock wedged between the seat and the door.

After Mr. Walsh and Mr. Shapiro drove off, Cyrus Snell yelled at the crowd, "You ignorant rednecks. They'll get your land. You better take their offers, dumb-nuts!"

As they headed down the road, Lum noticed how dark the mountain range had become. She leaned against the cool window to numb the pain. A loud thunderclap sounded. Lightning flashed. She closed her eyes.

"Walter's a damn fool," Jimmy blurted. "He can't speak for me. I think we should talk to them men and just see what their offer is."

"You mean sell the farm?" Ethel asked.

"Look, we ain't getting no younger. Can't hardly make it now. With the price of feed, we barely make a penny selling hogs no more." He stared out the windshield.

Ethel said, "Things'll get better, don't you think?"

"Ain't got no reason to think that."

"We was planning on leaving the farm to Junior."

"Why? So he can struggle like us? He might do better getting work with this Scenic. I bet they'd hire him. He's almost sixteen. Let's go tomorrow to the Resettlement Office and talk to them. Don't say nothing to Walter."

"Jimmy," Lum interrupted. "That's our land! Don't you remember Daddy always said to keep it in the family?"

"Of course, but Daddy don't know what it's like now. I hate having to sell, but you heard Cyrus. He said they'd take our land like it or not. I aim to get in on the ground floor while they still have money."

Lum said, "You gotta get all us to agree. It's not just your decision."

"Me and Jimmy and Walter been working the farm, not you." Ethel glared at her.

"I've helped you out when you needed me. How about all them hogs I helped with?"

"Lum," Jimmy said, "I'm gonna talk to them men and if they give me a good offer I won't make no decision 'til all the family agree, including my boys. Just don't say nothing to Al, neither. I don't want him and Walter messing this up."

"Fine. Just keep me in mind. What am I gonna do if we decide to sell?"

"Yeah," Ethel said, "I don't want to work in no factory."

"How hard can it be? We'll get a new house and won't have to worry all the time like we do now," Jimmy said. "We may even get enough to not have to work, like them other men."

"You're fooling yourself if you think that," Ethel said. "We'll work until we can't no more. I'm going with you to talk to them men."

A pair of headlights pulled up close behind them, then an engine roared and a long brown car passed them on the curvy road.

"Snell," muttered Jimmy.

Pain thumped above Lum's eyebrow. She closed her eyes again, resting her forehead against her hand. She just wanted to climb into bed and not have to think about anything or listen to Ethel's voice.

On Sundays She Does It All

1920

Every morning Lum would get Granny dressed. The old woman stayed in bed, but she wanted to be washed and clothed by daybreak. Lum and Granny ate breakfast together in silence. Granny's smile or frown could convey more than words. Lum welcomed the quiet, so she could think about the day, what she'd cook, imagining picking vegetables in the sunny patch.

Sometimes she'd rehearse having conversations with her dolls. She had Bunny still, even at nineteen, and two dolls. One was made by Amy, who brought a cloth doll when she'd helped with Lum's birth. The other one she got when she turned five. She still remembered that birthday. She'd been sick with the chicken pox and had to stay away from everyone. Daddy brought her present to her bed, and she hugged the doll all through her sickness. She talked to Francie, the doll, since no one visited her except Granny, who brought chicken soup. When Lum was seven, Two Pint had pulled all the golden hair from the doll's head, but Lum still loved her and would take scraps of cloth to make colorful scarves to cover the bald head with holes where the strands had been.

When she wasn't washing Granny, cooking, or cleaning, she was helping Ethel with her children, Junior, Sally, and Raymond. June and the other cousins would come to see Granny, but as her condition lingered, they came less and less.

Ethel worked a lot, too, so Lum didn't feel resentful, although Ethel was jealous of the closeness of her children to Lum. Especially Raymond. He clung to her, being the baby of the family. She often held him in her lap as she snapped beans or shelled peas. When June brought her brood the first couple of times, Margaret would try to push Raymond off of Lum's lap. Seeing Margaret clinging to Lum, June scolded her, saying, "Go watch after your sisters and brother." After that, only June came to visit Granny, leaving Margaret home to babysit. Lum's caregiving had shifted from the very young to the very old.

One Sunday, Lum convinced Ethel to stay with Granny so Lum could go to church. Instead of sitting with her father and brothers, she sat with June's family. Margaret snuggled up to Lum. Margaret's hair smelled so clean that Lum held the little girl close, her nose in the rose-scented hair.

"Lum, why don't you come over for Sunday dinner?" June asked when the service was over.

"Oh, I'd love to, but Ethel . . ."

"Let Ethel cook her own dinner. We all miss you something awful."

"I miss you-all too." Lum bent over and gathered Margaret, Elsie, Bertha, and Robbie to her. They had grown so much since she'd left two years earlier. As much as she loved Granny and Daddy and the boys, living with June had been much easier. She remembered putting up bread and butter pickles with June. "You still have some of those pickles?"

"Sure do. We could have some if you like." June looked up at Lum with hopeful eyes. Lum's father and brothers were talking with the other farmers. Daddy always wanted dinner at one. Usually Lum stayed home to cook so dinner would be ready when they returned from church. Maybe Ethel would have dinner ready. "Let me go talk to Jimmy."

Jimmy was talking with Al and Walter when Lum approached the group, already tasting bread and butter pickles.

"Jimmy, you think Ethel will have dinner ready?"

He looked at her. "Well, you usually help her."

"Not on Sundays. I do it all." She hesitated, hating to ask a favor. "I'm just wondering, if I walked with June and them and maybe got home a little later, if that would be all right. You know, so Daddy will still have dinner on time."

"I don't know, Lum. Maybe you should've asked her before we left home."

"I din't think about it then. June asked me to dinner, but I didn't think y'all would like it much."

He grunted. "Lum, I think we can do without you for one Sunday dinner. You go on and be with June and them."

She could do what she wanted! Her shoulders felt lighter as she joined June and her husband and children. She held hands with Margaret and Elsie all the way to June's. Margaret tried to shoo Elsie away, but Lum insisted that she had two hands and Elsie could hold one of them. Youthful energy seeped into Lum's hands, wrists, and forearms, and she felt like a school girl again.

Margaret helped June and Lum prepare dinner and informed her sisters that "me and Lum fried the chicken" since Margaret put the pieces Lum had cut up into a bowl of buttermilk and then into a paper bag with flour and salt and pepper. Margaret had held the bag out to Lum so she could arrange the chicken pieces into the large cast iron pan.

"Margaret, you are such a big and helpful girl, will you help your mama wash the dishes so I can get on home to clean up there?"

She had nodded with tears trickling down her cheeks.

When Lum reached the farm, Jimmy ran up to her. "Ethel's about to strangle you. You go in there and apologize before she has a chance to say anything."

"Jimmy," she said, incredulous. "You're the one told me it would be all right to go to June's."

"I said you should'a asked her beforehand."

"You did, but then you said to go on, that you-all could do without me for one dinner."

He shook his head. "She hadn't even started dinner because she was taking care of Granny and nursing Raymond."

"I do all that." Then she blushed. Of course she didn't nurse a baby. "And I still have dinner by the time you all come home."

"Didn't work out that way."

"Did you even tell your wife . . . ?"

"Women's work is between women." He strode toward the fields a little faster than he usually walked.

Scaredy-cat, thought Lum. *He's afraid of his own wife. And for good reason.* Ethel screeched when Lum entered the kitchen door, "Where the blue blazes you been? Your daddy is furious about dinner. I had Raymond and Granny, and where were you?"

"I was . . ."

"I know where you was. The question is, why the dickens you thought you could get out of your duties here."

"I asked Jimmy, and he said . . ."

"Puh! Don't you know? Never ask a man. He don't know what all we do. What all *I* have to do around here."

"Ethel. Before I come back here, you were handling everything."

"I had Granny, you fool!" Ethel pointed to the table with dirty dishes. "Taking care of a baby ain't easy, but you add in two young'uns and three men and an old woman who cain't get out of bed, what do you think?"

"I'm sorry, but I . . ."

Ethel turned her back on Lum and started picking up dishes.

I do as much if not more, Lum thought as she helped Ethel in silence. She hurried so she could be out of the anger-filled kitchen and could be with Granny, where the silence was welcome, not hostile.

A Different Kind of Mad

1933

Lum's temple throbbed against the glass, and she wished Ethel would stop chattering about the meeting. Whenever the truck shook, Lum's head would bounce against the window, but she was almost grateful for the pain since it was a different hurt from the persistent stabbing above her eye. Finally, they lurched to a full stop. Lum spied the farmhouse through the rain-streaked pane. Jimmy pulled as close as he could to the granite steps, but Lum's foot still landed in a deep puddle. Once on the porch, she looked longingly at the little room, but knew she had to see Margaret first. She dreaded telling her Al had gone to the roadhouse.

Quietness pervaded the house, so Lum peeked around corners for Margaret or Meg. They were asleep on Margaret's bed, Meg's wispy ginger hair next to Margaret's darker locks. She envied their peaceful sleep. All she wanted was a dark, silent place. The wet shoe squeaked as she left the room. At least she didn't come home to an angry Margaret.

In her own room, she lay with the cool sheet against the right side of her head, her shawl rolled up under her neck. The pain pounded her into the bed, and she imagined the mattress absorbing it. Once Amy had given her some dried feverfew for a headache, but it didn't take long for Lum to use it all. Maybe a little of the paregoric would help. At least she could sleep. "Infant use only," she had repeated. A promise. Meg needed it more than she did. Or did she? At that moment she couldn't be sure.

Turning over, the painful side exposed to the air, she prayed for an end to the pain. She hadn't needed to go to that meeting. The Snells had tried to keep her out, but she had persisted. Now look what happened. Probably being around all that yelling was what caused the headache. Cyrus Snell seemed to always be looking out just for himself. She bet he wasn't troubled by headaches or doubts of conscience. And sure as rain, he'd benefit from this road or else he wouldn't be so chummy with those strangers.

Footfalls sounded across the porch. Lum braced herself for Margaret's anger when she heard knuckles against the door.

"Aunt Lum," Caleb called. "Aunty Lum?"

"Come in." When she pulled herself to a sitting position, pain pounded anew.

He stuck his head around the door. "Aren't we gonna have supper?"

"Oh, sweetie, I just saw your mama and Little Meg a-sleeping, so I came in to lay down a minute." She pushed her swollen feet into soggy shoes. "Let's go find you something to eat. You must be starving."

"Kinda hungry," he agreed, holding the door open for her.

Lum heated some bacon grease in a cast iron pan, threw together some cornmeal, eggs, baking powder, and milk, poured the mixture into the heated pan and closed the oven. She dumped canned okra and tomatoes into a pan all together, added chunks of hoop cheese and chopped onion. Caleb swore he hated okra until Lum had fixed it this way one time. She set a crock of pickled beans on the table and sliced some ham.

"See if your mama wants to come eat," she suggested to Caleb, who was playing with his pocketknife. She suspected he was making tiny cuts in the table edge, but whenever she looked, he spun the knife around in his hand. Although she'd like to let Margaret stay asleep, she had to give her the chance to join them. She hoped Margaret would say she wasn't hungry, but if Lum didn't ask, Margaret would hold it against her. While Caleb was out of the kitchen, she held the cold Ball jar against her aching head.

"She says let her know when dinner's ready," Caleb reported

"It'll be just a minute 'til the cornbread's done." Lum ran water into the Ball jar and watched the bits of tomatoes come loose from its sides. Caleb's boots resounded through the house as he retrieved his stepmother. While Lum was concentrating on the swirling water, Margaret sat down, her back as stiff as her lips.

"Oh, Margaret, I didn't want to wake you. You and the baby were sleeping so good." She placed the full jar in the sink.

"Mmm."

"Al asked me to tell you he was going to the roadhouse. Not to wait up."

Margaret's lips pressed inward.

"Margaret?" Lum tentatively spoke. "I went to this meeting in town. Al and Jimmy and Walter and even Ethel all were there."

Margaret looked at the opposite wall.

Lum stood directly in front of her. "You mad?"

Not a word.

Since the cornbread smelled done, Lum took it out of the oven. The throbbing increased when she bent over. After testing with a knife to see if it was done, then slicing it like a pie, she placed it in front of Margaret.

"Sit down, Caleb," Lum directed. "Sorry about supper being late. They were telling us about the road."

Caleb asked where the road was going, so Lum told as much as she knew and a little bit about the meeting. She couldn't tell Caleb everything because she didn't want him to know how his daddy and the other men had acted.

"I could get me a job working on the road." Caleb sopped up tomato juice with cornbread.

"Your daddy wouldn't like that. You best stay in school."

"You don't know what Daddy wants," he snapped. "I could make money. Daddy's always saying we don't have enough. Joe Earl quit school to work, and he gets paid good."

"Your daddy's mad about that road, so I don't think you should ask him just yet, honey. More ham?"

"Yes, ma'am." He scraped the remaining slices onto his plate.

She wished Margaret would say something. She'd pass vegetables if asked, but otherwise she was mum as a dung beetle. Lum hated when people were mad but wouldn't say anything. She'd rather Margaret fuss at her for being late or letting Al miss supper, whatever she was mad about. Lum tried to concentrate on popping little round okra seeds with her teeth, but her forehead still had the feeling of an ice pick plunged deep inside. After Caleb finished eating and had left the room, Lum said, "I'm boiling some herbs for Meg. She been colicky today? Mr. Reeves didn't want to sell me any paregoric and he made me promise to keep it away from Al." Lum fumbled in her neckline and brought out the rumpled bag.

Margaret pulled the sack toward herself.

Lum stacked the dirty dishes and carried them to the sink. "I asked Mr. Reeves if he's seen Al with anybody, but all he mentioned was Kenny." She lifted the cast iron pot from the stove, poured boiling water over the dishes, and added a bar of lye soap, swishing it around. Since Margaret didn't want to talk, Lum decided to just hurry up cleaning the kitchen and lie back down. That was the only way to get rid of this kind of headache. Quiet and darkness. When her granny had a headache she used to put a flour sack over her head.

Tonight Lum wouldn't feel like pulling out the cards. The Fat Lady would be on the train to Pittsburgh, looking out the window, not knowing what would happen in the new sideshow or where she would be living next. Her little trailer had been fixed up so nice, especially with the flowered curtains she'd made, but the manager hadn't let her take anything out of the trailer except her clothes. Just because the manager's wife didn't like her, she'd been sold to another sideshow. The wife, formerly a show girl, was mean, so at least the Fat Lady wouldn't have to put up with that kind of treatment any longer. Oh, but she'd miss the twins—"Daisy and Violet, Violet and Daisy, Daisy and Violet," the train tracks intoned. The words reverberated in Lum's forehead.

"It's some floozy at that roadhouse."

The Fat Lady's train ride ended. Was Margaret talking to herself? Or to her?

"Least you could'a done is follow him down there. You swore you'd find out."

"But I thought you'd want me here. With the paregoric. For supper."

Margaret let out a loud sigh and pushed away from the table. "All I ask is one little thing. But no, you linger around town and don't even find out what I asked."

"But . . ."

Margaret was already gone.

Hangover Tea
1933

The absence of pain woke Lum. It was still dark, but she didn't know what time it was without a clock in her room. Gingerly, she touched her forehead. Only a shadow of pain remained. She rubbed her hand across her chin, feeling sharp stubble. She'd have to shave early in the morning since she'd gone straight to bed last night after washing dishes. She hadn't even taken her dress off. Just her shoes. Lum wondered why Margaret had been so cold to her, since Lum hadn't done anything wrong. It wasn't possible to find out in one day if Al was stepping out and, if so, who with.

The Fat Lady would have stayed in her seat since the train aisle was so narrow. She'd have eaten a whole fried chicken, six biscuits, a jar of pickled green tomatoes, and half an apple pie. Lum wondered how carnival people ate. Did they have a traveling cook? What would it be like to cook for such interesting people and go from town to town? Was the cook sorry or glad to see the Fat Lady go? If it meant less cooking, probably yes. But maybe every day the Fat Lady told the cook how much she enjoyed the food. When people love your cooking, it doesn't matter how much you have to make.

Bright lights shone in her window. It had to be Al's truck. Now was her chance to find out some news. She pulled the shawl around her shoulders and ventured onto the porch. Al was stepping carefully through the steady drizzle, eyes cast toward the ground. She settled into a rocking chair so he wouldn't know she got up for him. He jerked his head up when he saw her.

"Lum!" He started. "What you doing up?"

"I had a mighty bad headache and went to bed early, but I woke up in the middle of the night. Now I can't get back to sleep."

Al groaned. "Bet I'll wake up with a doozy of a headache."

"Let me make you some hangover tea."

"Is there such a thing?"

"You drink a cup of my special tea before bed, and you'll wake up fresh." Pushing down on the armrests, she stood. "Come on and let me fix you up so you can sleep."

Al grinned. "You're the doctor."

In the kitchen, Al sat at the table while Lum gathered some ash from the bottom of the stove, since the burnt wood was willow, mixed it with molasses, and added boiling water. "Jimmy and Walter swear by this," she said, handing him the cup.

Al sniffed the creation. "I always heard nothing cured like hair of the dog that bit you."

"That just prolongs it. Less'n you intend to drink all day and night."

"Not a bad idea, but only if it makes you forget your life."

She settled in next to Al at the table. "Your life as bad as all that?"

"Not if it stayed the same as it used to be." He sipped the tea. "Kinda gritty."

"When was the best time for you?"

"Oh, let's see. When I was young and running around. I'd work hard all week, and I had Sunday off. Back then I wasn't worrying about nothing. Now I'm always anxious about the farm—how can I keep my family fed, sell enough milk and eggs, keep the farm going? On top of all that, I might lose the farm. In Daddy's day, times weren't so hard."

"Times were hard, Al, but your daddy was doing the worrying, not you. Don't you think it's all part of being grown up?"

"I reckon." Al shrugged. "Braxton Snell showed up at the road-house. He was trying to listen in on what we was talking about, so we invited him to join us. After a few shots of liquor, he started bragging about how much he and his daddy are gonna make off this damn road. There's all these rules about who can have a business for tourists so not just anybody can open an inn. You gotta put up $30,000 or something, but they're making an exception for the Snells since they sold so much of their own land and are gonna help get everybody else to sell. He's putting up a hunting lodge for the tourists. He said we could come up there to hunt if we sold our land."

Lum snorted. "Huh!"

"That's what I thought, too. Any time them people are nice to you, you can bet they're trying to get something out of you." He drank some more of Lum's mixture and grimaced. "He said we better take their offer or it won't be pretty."

"What's that mean?"

"He said they have their ways of getting what they want, so we better sell now."

"But what would you do?" Lum asked, thinking, *What would* I *do?*

"He didn't change my mind none. All I know is farming. Daddy'd sit up in his coffin and spit if he knew I'd done sold the farm. I want Caleb to run it when he's grown. All them Yankees want it for is for folks to stop their cars and look out over the valley. They can do that anywhere. If I don't sell, they'll just find another place for that." He gulped some tea. "But I invited Braxton to supper next Friday. He loves to talk about all the money he thinks he's gonna make. You fix a real good meal, and we'll see what else we can find out from him."

She'd make a good supper, but she dreaded having to listen to all that Snell boasting.

Sides

1933

What a restless night, Lum thought as the sun streamed into her room. She and Al had stayed up half the night talking. Margaret had to be wrong about the supposed girlfriend. Only one thing on that man's mind: his farm. He felt he'd be failing generations before him and his son if he lost the land. She started feeling the old resentment caused by losing her part of the family farm because she was a woman. Her brothers and other family members tried to make her feel they were being charitable for sharing their homes with her. She, who did so much work for them. Speaking of work, she wanted to make some pancakes served with good thick bacon and sorghum syrup. She was hungry since she hadn't felt like eating the night before.

Since she could see her breath in the little room, she pulled on thick cotton stockings and her heaviest dress. When she stepped off the granite steps, she noticed that puddles remained. Whipped by the wind, corn stalks crackled. Was this the last year for a corn crop? Would cars be driving where the cornrows stood? What would childhood be like for Meg without getting lost in the rows of corn, tall stalks brushing against arms, being chased by roosters, and planting seeds in spring, summers spent picking beans, autumn canning? Margaret said children worked in mills. Did they get to stop work and go to school in the winter? Several families she'd known had left for mill towns, but she'd never heard anything from them afterwards.

A car drove up the wet road with Mr. Shapiro behind the wheel. She supposed he was going up to meet with Kenny and try to talk the Portugee out of their homes. She couldn't imagine those sangers and moonshiners in some town. They knew these woods like she knew the inside of her apron pocket, but they had only a scrap of land and most likely didn't have deeds. Could the Portugee and Mr. Shapiro even understand each other? Some of them talked in that old-fashioned kind of speech. Those mountain people could hold a grudge for generations.

"Good morning, chickies," she sang out in a high-pitched voice, entering the chicken coop, so that mean old rooster could strut himself on out of there. "Got some eggs for me today?" Every morning was a discovery—what color eggs she would find. Brown eggs from the Dominickers, pinkish brown from the Delawares? Leghorns were always white. After gathering eggs in her apron, she headed to the springhouse for buttermilk.

Back in the kitchen, she breathed in the aroma of ground coffee. Oh, it was the smell she loved more than the taste. She measured scoops into the pot with cold spring water. She quickly made a pancake batter while the bacon cooked. The batter sizzled when it met the hot bacon fat in the cast iron frying pan. She scooped butter out of the mold onto a plate and set the table, returning to the stove in time to flip the pancakes.

"Morning, Lum," Al boomed. "No hangover! You should patent that potion you fixed up last night and make a million dollars. Aunty Lum's Sure Fire Hangover Remedy."

She guffawed. "That'd be okay long as you don't try to put my picture on the bottle," she said, thinking of Good Old Granny Graybill's Pine Tar Remedy with a stern-looking crone on the label. She was pleased to be responsible for his good mood, but remembered how cold Margaret had been late last night. "Margaret up?"

"Getting dressed." He plopped down at the table. "Coffee ready?"

"In a minute." She flipped some pancakes on a plate, added bacon, and set it in front of him. "Here's some syrup."

Margaret shuffled in, hair looking like a fox had died on her head.

"Good morning," Lum called out, not too loudly or too cheerily, in fear she might be chastised, or worse, ignored.

"Mmm."

Oh, here we go again. Will she give me the cold shoulder all day?

"Coffee's ready," she announced to the still air, poured out three cups, and put two on the table.

Margaret sat across from Al. "You want to tell me where you was at last night?"

"Didn't Lum tell you? I went to the roadhouse." Al scooped sugar into his cup.

"Yeah, she told me. But why you using her for your messenger?"

"After that meeting some of the boys wanted to go talk things over." Al shoved a forkful of hotcakes into his mouth.

"Boys, huh?"

Standing, Lum silently sipped her coffee. She usually added sugar, but if she went to the table to get some, she'd interrupt the line of fire, and Margaret's anger might be directed at her.

When Al finished chewing, he said, "Can't I enjoy my breakfast without your harping?"

"But you was out so late."

Al pushed back from the table, gulped down his coffee, glared at Margaret. "If I want to go out at night, that's my business." He stomped out the kitchen door.

Margaret stared into her coffee even when Lum set a plate of pancakes in front of her.

"I don't think there's another woman," Lum said. "Al's so worried about losing his land, I don't think he could concentrate on a woman if one flew in his face."

"So now you're on his side?"

"There are no sides, Margaret. I love you both. Remember when you got married and the preacher turned to the congregation and asked us to pledge to help keep the marriage together? That was a solemn oath, and I stand by it."

Margaret grunted and cut a pancake with her fork edge. After a few minutes she said, "You going to town today?"

"If it's all right with you." When Margaret didn't respond, she added, "Need anything?"

"I don't know about you going to town every day and getting home so late."

"If you want, I can tell Liza I can't do it no more."

"Well, it's just . . ." Margaret stopped, seeing Caleb walk in.

"Good morning, honey. We have pancakes." Lum returned to the griddle.

"Oh, boy!"

What was Margaret about to say? Would this be my last day of chicken soup and a walk to town? Lum gave Caleb a plate and prepared one for herself. She drenched the pancakes with sorghum, careful to keep the bacon slices out of the syrup. She liked to finish a sweet meal with salty bacon. Margaret's remarks threatened to ruin a good breakfast.

"Hurry up, Caleb, so you won't be late to school." Margaret finished her coffee.

"Why do I have to go? I ain't learning nothing I need to know. I could be working at the quarry like Joe Earl."

"Don't you say that to your daddy," Margaret warned. "He don't want you working at no quarry. Daddy needs you a-helping on the farm."

"Folks say the road's going right through everybody's farm. Ain't gonna be no farms left." He turned a hard face to Lum. "And you said so, Aunt Lum."

"Farmers are being offered money to sell, but your daddy's not selling," Lum said. "Anyway, nobody ever regretted getting educated, but lots of folks are sorry they didn't finish school." She hoped Caleb wouldn't end up working in a mill. Not as a child or an adult.

"Get on ready, Caleb. Lum'll walk down there with you."

"I don't need her walking me to school."

Well, Lum thought, *it sounds like I will be going to Mr. Shay's today.* When Caleb left the room, Margaret said, "Why don't you go on for one more day, and we'll decide if you should keep on helping him. You must get tired going back and forth."

"It's not too much," Lum protested. It was a lot of walking, but she liked earning money. And she liked not having to do anything while he slept.

"We'll talk tonight. You get on now, I want you to make sure Caleb goes to school. I'll clean up the dishes."

The Company of Women

1927

All through her childhood, Margaret kept Lum special, bragging all the time how "me and Lum" did such and so. After Granny died and Ethel and Jimmy's children were old enough to help out, Lum wasn't needed very much, only at harvest season. Sometimes she was sent to care for an old uncle or aunt when one was feeling poorly, but she spent most of her time with Cousin June's family, sharing a bed with Margaret. On Saturdays, Margaret and Lum would go to Lum's family farm. And Al and his wife, Mary Ellen, brought six-year-old Caleb.

Lum and Margaret were shucking corn while Ethel and Mary Ellen shelled peas. Lum enjoyed the time with the women, and teenaged Margaret had a break from watching her younger siblings. Lum heard Walter and Al laughing loudly while sipping moonshine, sitting on the tailgate of Al's truck. After she finished shucking an ear, Margaret wandered to the truck, although, Lum noted, there was still a pile of corn waiting. She was astounded that Margaret was standing by the truck chatting with the men when there was still work to be done.

As they were washing the dishes later, Lum told Margaret, "You shouldn't be talking with Walter and Al but with us women."

Margaret turned to her. "Why? They're more interesting."

"What's so interesting?"

"They talk about Two Pint and Tommy Lee and even Guthrie sometimes."

Lum knew Margaret had her there. She couldn't say to not listen to stories about her brothers. She wished to talk to Walter about them, but he wouldn't say anything, especially anything about the war. The oldest and youngest, Tommy Lee and Two Pint, died the same year. Tommy Lee didn't make it back from the war. Guthrie had refused to go in the army and the town had turned against him. There were rumors about Guthrie and some of the married women left behind, and almost as soon as Jimmy and Walter returned, Guthrie left. No one knew where he went, and he was never heard from again. Poor Two Pint complained because he wasn't old enough to enlist, but he died before the war ended when he got the flu in 1918. Sick one day and dead by nightfall, he was only 14.

Week after week, Margaret would slip away from the women's circle to be with Walter and Al. Mary Ellen was quiet, but Lum watched her watch Margaret. Lum felt like she spent so much of her life observing people, trying to figure out what they were thinking so she could please them. But she didn't know how to either make Mary Ellen feel better or keep Margaret from the men.

"That Margaret loves to talk," Lum said. "As long as somebody listens to her, she's happy."

"Hmm." Mary Ellen stared across the yard at her husband, her blond curls glistening in the afternoon sun. "Not everybody wants to hear her yammering."

"True. I tried telling her, but she's willful."

"That's one word for it." In high school, Mary Ellen had never been friendly with Lum, but when she started dating Al, she would occasionally speak to Lum in the hallways and even asked her for help with math. Maybe this was a chance for them to become closer, Lum hoped.

At dinnertime, Mary Ellen ate a little bit of potatoes and gravy, then got up and left the table.

"This happens at home a lot," Al confided. "She has trouble keeping food down. Can't swallow." Several minutes later she came back a little red-faced, hair tucked behind her ears. Al said, "Feel better, hon?"

She nodded and ate a little more slowly, leaving the beef on her plate.

After this happened a few more times, Lum anticipated hearing that Mary Ellen was expecting, but no announcement of another baby came.

Then Mary Ellen quit coming on Saturdays, and Al said she hadn't been feeling well. Lum noticed Margaret wasn't paying as much attention to Walter as she was to Al, and when Jimmy insisted on Walter's help, Al would entertain Margaret with his stories. The way her young cousin laughed, Lum figured they weren't talking about her brothers or the war. Lum knew only too well how Margaret could attach herself to someone. Looked like that someone was now Al. How dare she flirt—because that's what it looked like to Lum—with a married man?

After supper, when Al and Caleb had left, Lum and Margaret were sitting on the front porch in rocking chairs. Lum enjoyed looking at the cattle grazing. There was something so relaxing about them. She hated to chide Margaret, but what she was doing just wasn't right.

"Margaret, it doesn't look right, you hanging on to Al."

"Oh, we're just funning. I'm trying to cheer him up. He's sad about Mary Ellen being so sick." Margaret started rocking faster and Lum slowed her own chair, thinking she might have been wrong about Margaret.

"How sick is she? Does he say?"

Margaret frowned. "Pretty sick." She looked into the darkening sky. "He says she don't get out of bed most days. He has to get Caleb dressed and fed."

"Has the doctor come to see her?"

Margaret shrugged. "Al says the doctor don't know what's wrong with her."

"Maybe your mama and me could carry some food up there for Al and Caleb. I could make her some broth. Maybe she can keep that down."

"I'll ask Mama." Margaret kept rocking, but Lum stopped. She squinted into the field. The Black Angus cows were getting harder to see as the sun had disappeared behind the mountains. She pitied Al. He seemed to love Mary Ellen. They had been together since high school and married right before Al joined the Navy. She felt bad that she had chastised Margaret for "funning" with Al. He certainly needed cheering up. And nothing did that better than food.

Lum made extra food at June's, and Margaret insisted on

accompanying her in Walter's wagon up to Al's farm. Lum was feeding Mary Ellen some broth when she heard Walter, Al, and Margaret laughing.

"That's enough," Mary Ellen said, holding up her hand.

"You need to eat. I know you can't keep solid food down, but you can at least eat soup."

"Maybe you could leave the soup here and I'll eat later."

"Will Al help you with it?"

Mary Ellen nodded. Her once pretty hair was plastered to her head.

"When's the . . . I'm sorry to ask this, but when's the last time you had a bath?"

"Oh, I don't know. I just don't have the get up and go."

"Why don't I come back tomorrow and bathe you?"

"Oh, Lum." A tear glistened on Mary Ellen's cheek. "You'd do that for me?"

"Of course." Lum had washed Granny in her bed and knew it could be done without disturbing the ill person.

Mary Ellen grabbed Lum's hand. "Promise me. After I'm gone, make sure Al has a good wife. A *good* one. One who will love Caleb and make Al a comfortable home."

"Hush now, you're not . . ."

Mary Ellen interrupted her. Mary Ellen was not an interrupter. "Please listen. Al won't. I know I won't be here much longer. Take care of Al. Don't let him marry a flibbertigibbet."

"I promise." But really, she knew Al would marry whoever he wanted and wouldn't ask her permission.

A week later, she started staying at Al's since it was easier for her to cook at the house, and she would be there all day in case Mary Ellen or Caleb needed her. She loved Al's farm up the mountain where the air was cooler and she could look over the whole valley. Al often left at night and came in late. She could hear him coming home, sometimes near dawn, from the room she shared with Caleb. He was a sweet little boy who liked to cuddle. Lum missed the afternoons of being in the company of women. She'd talk to Mary Ellen, but Al's wife got thinner and thinner except for a distended stomach that seemed more prominent the more weight she lost. She could hardly eat anything other than broth and sometime she couldn't even keep that down. Doctor Miles came twice to see her and said he wasn't sure what was wrong, but left some tonic. It kept her from vomiting, but also made her drowsy. A couple of times when Al went to town he picked up some more tonic, but sometimes when Lum looked for the bottle she couldn't find it.

After Lum had been there for a year, Mary Ellen died. For a week afterwards Al seemed to do nothing but sleep, but then he was back to normal running the farm while Lum took care of Caleb and all the other chores. In late summer, when she gathered canning jars from the cellar, Lum found four empty tonic bottles hidden behind the sauerkraut urn.

Lum had always gotten along with Al, so she assumed she would stay on there. And she did. June's house had seemed easy compared with her former home, where Ethel now ruled, but living with Al and Caleb was the easiest. Walter sometimes came for supper, and she figured he must want to get away from Ethel. The two men friends would go out afterwards. Walter must be glad Al was a bachelor again even though he had a young son, Lum imagined.

He didn't stay a bachelor for long, probably *because* he had a son. Ethel had told Lum that people at church were starting to talk about her living with Al. Lum had to chuckle because Al was like a brother. The idea that the two of them—well, she had to laugh. So when he married Margaret, Lum's favorite of all the children she had cared for, she felt that she was finally secure and could continue on there.

After Margaret and Al were married for a few months, Lum noticed that Margaret was not as happy as she had been. Whenever she started a pout because she couldn't get her way, Al would tickle his wife in the ribs, causing her to laugh and slap at him. Lum had always hated being tickled that way, and she had to leave the room if he did it to Margaret in front of her. The sight of Margaret pinned down made Lum nauseated.

"It's hard," Margaret confided. "He already has his own house and his own ways and that woman's ways of running the house." She always referred to Mary Ellen as "that woman."

Lum thought, *But I've been running this house for a long time. She's really rejecting my ways.* Before long, Ethel asked Lum to come back and help her with the harvesting. "Just for fall and winter," Ethel said. "Then you can go back to Al's iffen you're wanting to."

She did want to, but after six months with Margaret's moodiness, she'd be ready for Ethel and her bossiness.

News

1933

When Lum crossed the town square she saw people gathered around the old law office, which, she now realized, was inhabited by the Resettlement Administration. She kept hearing "Snell" and "Don't know if he'll live."

Something must have happened to Mr. Snell after the meeting. She remembered how he'd sped past Jimmy's truck. Did his car go off the slippery road? She approached the crowd and asked, "What y'all talking about?"

"It's Mr. Snell." An old woman turned to her. "Got run over."

"After the meeting." A farmer's enormous stomach pushed against his overalls.

A voice said, "Smiley Hawkins in jail."

Lum asked, "What did Smiley do?"

"Tried to kill Mr. Snell," a young man said.

Impossible. Smiley wouldn't hurt anybody, not even someone who had beat him. At least she hoped not. And how could he if he was lame? There had to be a good explanation. People all started talking at once, saying that Mr. Snell had gotten trapped under that lawyer's car with Smiley in it. Lum remembered Cyrus Snell after the meeting insulting the farmers.

When she reached the Shays' house, Dan flung open the front door. "About time you got here. Tell me all about this meeting. And what happened to Cyrus Snell?"

"How did you know?" She noticed he had shaved.

"Liza said she saw you going in the church last night."

Standing in the hall, Lum told him about the meeting and what she'd heard about Snell.

"But did he do anything to make anybody want to kill him?"

"Well, he did call us dirty names when he left. He was going awful fast down the highway. But I heard it was Mr. Harper, the lawyer, and some colored men who ran over him. None of them was there last night."

"So it was a trap."

"How?" Taking a look at him, she thought his coloring looked good. "You seem to be feeling better."

He coughed in response, pulling the robe closer around his chest.

"You've had breakfast?"

"Some oatmeal. I could drink some coffee." His eyes were lively.

"Well, come on to the kitchen. Some mullein will clear up your lungs."

"Oh, don't make that stuff. I want coffee."

"Coffee won't help you none." Lum draped her shawl over a chair back.

"Maybe later some medicine-y tea." He winked.

He *was* feeling better. "I'll make coffee long as you promise not to put milk in it."

"It's no good without some cream, but you're the boss. Probably know more than that quack Meadows."

Dr. Meadows had replaced Dr. Miles but he was almost as old. People still thought of him as a newcomer who didn't measure up to Dr. Miles. Lum avoided all doctors. She hadn't had an illness that she couldn't cure with Amy's medicines, or Granny's remedies, or with the help of *Gunn's Domestic Medicine.*

While the coffee perked, Dan pestered her with questions about the road and how much the government offered Al.

"There isn't enough money in the world for him to sell his farm." Lum hadn't thought to ask Al how much the offer was. She'd been trained to not talk about money.

"Everybody has their price. Cyrus wasn't lying when he said the government has the right to take their land. You can object, but the government always wins." He sipped his coffee. "Ah, that feels good on my throat."

"Any hot liquid is soothing, but you need to clear up those lungs." *He's not so bad when he's in a good mood or wants information*, she thought. "So what do *you* think of the Scenic Highway?"

"It'll be the best thing ever happened to Granite Falls and the whole county. Hell, all of western Virginia! That road's gonna bring in business. People gotta sleep, and they gotta eat. I'm thinking about buying up some of these big old empty houses to start an inn or boarding house."

"Braxton Snell said you have to put up $30,000 to have an inn off the Scenic."

"Nonsense!" he exploded. "That's the most foolishest thing I ever heard!" He coughed, grabbed his napkin, hacked into it, then wheezed, trying to catch his breath.

Lum jumped up and got a glass of water. "Here, try to drink some water." *What violent reactions folks have to the Snells.*

He waved her away with one hand, the other over his mouth, rose, and went to the sink, spitting into the drain.

"Where's your medicine?"

"Already took it. This is what it's supposed to do. Expectorant," he blurted.

Such an appropriate word. His coughs sounded like tiny explosions. Once Dan quit spitting, he said he was exhausted, and went to bed.

Lum resolved to go by Amy's after Liza got home to find out if Smiley was really in jail. And Amy would have something for her to take in case one of her headaches came on again. Margaret was already mad about her coming home late, but it wouldn't take long to stop at the cabin for a minute.

Spying a long sack of onions, Lum decided to make some onion broth. She peeled and sliced, eyes burning. Onions that potent would make a good poultice. She wished she had a beef bone to add flavor. Dan must have plenty of money since he planned on buying houses. Not just one house; he had said "houses." She dug around the indoor icebox for a roast but couldn't find anything other than a plucked chicken and some fresh pork. Maybe, if she got to come back, she could cook some beans with the pork for a nice bean soup. She was starting to like this noontime soup routine. Staying here wasn't bad as long as Dan kept sleeping most of the day. If Margaret planned on telling her she had to stay at the farm and not help the Shays, couldn't Lum make her own decision? She stirred the fragrant soup, mixing the little bubbles on the side until it came to a full boil, then lowered it to a simmer.

While the broth cooked, she read the *Washington Post* but saw nothing about the Scenic Highway. Even the crime stories she usually found interesting seemed humdrum. If only Granite Falls had a daily paper, she could find out the truth about Mr. Snell and Smiley. The weekly paper included who had been arrested, but it wouldn't come out until Friday. She decided to venture outside.

In the small garden everything drooped from last night's rain. Branches lay scattered about the backyard, and a large camellia was surrounded by its blooms, blown to the ground. *The Shays are obviously happy with a little yard*, she thought, remembering what Walter had said about little houses and little yards at the meeting. *What an easy life Liza must have. After teaching all day she comes home, makes dinner out of a small garden, and has money to buy things at the store. If she wants canned vegetables, she buys them.*

Lum's people had always had farms. But she was learning that she was adaptable. Didn't she have to be, since she had to fit in wherever she was taken? Each household had its own rules, such as when dinner and supper were fixed. She walked about, picking up branches to stack neatly by the back door, to be used as kindling after a few days of drying. The feel of crisp air following a storm reminded her of Dan's difficulties breathing. She'd better check on him.

When she peeked in the bedroom, she saw the outline of Dan's thin body facedown under a quilt. At least he knew to sleep on his stomach to reduce the chance of coughing. Seemed like whenever he started, it was difficult to stop.

She wandered back to the book-lined front room. Scanning the spines, she noticed a whale's tail. She pulled down the book, *Moby Dick*, and read about the young sailor forced to share a bed with a very strange person, unlike anyone she'd ever read about. She had cards picturing men who got tattoos to work in a sideshow, but Queequeg worked on ships. She settled into a comfortable chair and accompanied Ishmael to an odd church. The two men quickly felt love for each other and joined a whaling crew. She closed her eyes, book open on her chest. Kenny's blue eyes, peering out under black hair, came to mind. What is it about an ordinary person having feelings for a strange person?

"Hah!" A voice penetrated the silence. "Sleeping on the job, eh?"

Dan Shay stood in front of her, the bottom three buttons of his pajama top undone, a hairy paunch protruded at her eye level.

Startled, Lum struggled awake. "Oh, I was just . . . couldn't sleep last night."

He sniffed. "What's cooking? I'm sick of chicken soup."

"Onion broth. Thought it'd help break up your congestion."

"Well, dish it out, woman. Sleeping makes a man hungry."

For all his gruffness, Dan never treated her as anything other than a woman. He didn't know how to treat a woman kindly, but at least he saw her that way.

When he complimented her on the tasty broth, she protested, "It'd be a lot better if I had a beef bone."

Dan slurped soup. "What if I got a roast? You could make me some beef soup."

"I could." She nodded. "You'd have to be careful to not choke on the beef, though." She tapped her chin, thinking, *He doesn't want beef broth, he wants the meat.* She'd chop it up real small for him. She remembered her pan of fried onions.

"I'm gonna make you a poultice for your chest. I waited for you to get up so it'd be hot when I lay it on you."

He growled, "Just got up, and you're gonna make me lie down again?"

"I brought a flannel bag with a strap to keep it on your chest."

He sighed. "I just want to sit by the window and look for birds."

Lum dragged a chair by the back door so he could look at the backyard, hoping he'd notice how she'd picked up branches and swept.

"How come you never got married? Gal nice as you?"

Lum gritted her teeth. She hated getting that question. "Reckon nobody wanted me."

"There's somebody for everybody," he replied. "Go in the study and fetch my binoculars off the desk, would you?"

A layer of dust surrounded the green felt writing surface of the oak roll top desk. Stationery headed, "Daniel O'Connor Shay, Vice President, Staunton Building and Loan," sat in the middle next to an inkpot and fountain pen. A letter opener matching the fountain pen lay beside some envelopes with slit tops. The little cubbyholes were full of folded papers. Black binoculars were on the corner, large lens side down. She hurried back with them. While he stared through the binoculars, she scooped some lard into a cast iron pan and fried more onion slices. She wondered why, since the *Washington Post* was full of stories about bankers who lost all their money, Dan seemed to have plenty. Once the onions had softened, she added a handful of cornmeal to make a paste and packed it into a flannel pouch.

"Slip this around your neck and put the sack under your shirt." She held out the pouch. "It'll heat your lungs good."

He undid the top two buttons, leaving only one middle button still fastened, then, when he took the packet, yelled, "You're trying to burn me!"

"It won't burn," she scolded. "Just put it on your chest."

He did so and closed all the buttons. "I'm gonna step outside."

"Now why you want to do that? It's cold out there."

"But I got this to keep me warm."

"It's not good for you to get warm, then cold, then come back in the warm house."

"Stop babying me!" After opening the door, he asked, "What's this pile of sticks?"

"I tidied up the yard. You can use 'em for kindling when they dry out."

"You keep yourself busy, don't you? Here I thought you was reading and snoozing all day," he teased.

"Just picked up a book when I didn't see anything left to do. Didn't mean to fall asleep."

"Walk around the yard with me a bit. I get so tired of being inside. I gotta enjoy the sun when it makes an appearance."

"Careful of the puddles," she cautioned.

He walked slowly, one hand over the poultice. "What you think of *Moby Dick*?"

"Good so far."

"What you like about it?"

"It's so interesting—those two men, so different, but they love each other."

"Huh!" he seemed surprised. "And here I thought it was about a man chasing a whale. Liza couldn't never finish it. She said she just didn't care enough about whales. She liked those Brontë books better, especially *Jane Eyre*. She read it over and over."

"That's how I feel about *Little Women*. Must have read it a hundred times. It's the only fiction book I ever had when I was little. Granny left me a Bible and *Gunn's Domestic Medicine*."

"That where you learned about this mess you made me?"

"Not from *Gunn's*, though he does go on about flannel. My granny used to make it."

"Book I read over and over is *White Fang*. White Fang was all tore up with three bullet holes clear through him. He was given a one in *ten thousand* chance to live, and he did. I remember that when I face insurmountable tasks." He stopped. "Let's rest a minute."

"Don't overdo it. I bet even White Fang didn't recover in a day."

"It took him a long time." He looked up at the bare branches. "You know, you're not just some ignorant country woman. You're not at all like what people say."

Lum's heart raced. She was afraid to ask what folks said. "You ready to go back in?"

"I reckon."

When they climbed the back steps, she asked if the poultice was still warm. He nodded. "Go on and make some of that mullein tea you're always pushing on me."

She was wary of his niceness, anticipating the reappearance of the cranky Dan Shay. He said, "If you want, you can take *Moby Dick* with you. Long's you promise to bring it back."

"Oh, I don't have time to read at the farm. I'm busy from sun up to past dark. Besides..." She paused. Might as well bring this up now. "Tell the truth, I'm not sure Margaret's gonna let me come back tomorrow."

"What?" he thundered. "I've just gotten used to you."

"This morning she said it was too much—me getting home late—and she's gonna decide what I should do." She hoped he wouldn't have another coughing fit like when she mentioned Braxton Snell.

"You tell Margaret I need you."

"She needs help with her baby and cooking and all that."

"She had that baby, she can damn well take care of it. I'm sick!" He pointed to his chest. "You tell her if she doesn't let you come down here every day 'til I feel better, her son won't have a schoolteacher. I'm not breaking in no more granny women or maiden aunts. Only one to take care of me is Liza if you're not going to, even if the school has to close."

So he does want me to come back. Would he carry out his threat?

"I'll tell her." She didn't want to have to tell Margaret. Maybe if she went by Amy's and bought something for Meg's colic, Margaret would see how important it was for Lum to earn money. Heaven forbid Margaret would throw her out like that other time.

Nowhere to Go

1929

Caleb fell off the pasture gate right in front of Margaret and Lum, who were weeding around the tomatoes and peppers. He ran to Lum, who gathered him up and carried him into the room they shared to clean up his skinned elbow. She dabbed it with iodine and soothed him as he cried out from the sting. Margaret stood in the doorway, hands on her hips. Her lips were so tight together they almost disappeared.

"He din't come to me," Margaret said when they were alone.

"I was just closer," Lum said, hoping Margaret wouldn't start sulking.

"How's he gonna come to see me as his mama iffen you keep babying him?"

"You know how . . ." Lum paused, wondering how to say diplomatically that Margaret had favored her to her own mother when something like that happened to her. "Well, you always said I had a way with children." Margaret herself hadn't said that, but others had. Lum knew Margaret well enough to not say "other folks." That would inevitably lead Margaret to react badly. "You always loved me, you know."

Margaret stood up taller. "But not more than my own mama! You don't know how hard I try to get him to love me. But he just prefers you!" She slammed the kitchen door and stalked toward the pasture.

Should she follow after her? Best not to. Margaret would run to Al, who could calm her down. Lum wanted to go to Caleb, blow on his elbow, and tell him he'd feel better soon. No, she'd wait for Margaret to come back. If Margaret saw her with Caleb, she wouldn't forgive her for being kind.

Lum decided to mend some of Al's socks since she'd noticed holes in the heels when she washed them. She went outside to watch the sun dip toward the grey mountains. She enjoyed the layers of dark blue, light blue, then gray, fading into light gray. She held up the grey yarn against the top mountain range, squinting as it blended.

Al and Margaret strode toward her and then separated as Al headed to the water pump.

"What you doing now?" Margaret asked.

"Darning Al's socks."

Margaret frowned. "You're making me look like a bad wife."

"Don't be silly."

"Silly?" Margaret hissed.

"Margaret, I'm trying to help you out."

"Well, that's what you say, but I know you want Al for yourself."

"That's really silly . . ."

"Stop saying that!" Margaret hit her fist into her own palm.

"I'm sorry, I just want to help."

"Well, stop helping so much. We don't need all your help. Why don't you go back to Jimmy and Ethel's? They've got more young'uns than we do."

"You know it's not my time yet. Not until November."

"I'll say when it's time. Go pack up."

"What?" Margaret couldn't be serious. They'd had spats before, but Lum had never been told to leave.

"You're not deaf. You heard me. Al can take you down there while I make supper. And don't insult me by saying I can't make my family supper."

Lum balled up the socks with the needle still attached. *Margaret can just finish it herself since she's such a great wife*, she thought. As she passed through the kitchen, she dropped the socks on the table and proceeded to Caleb's room. He was playing with a little bear, holding his hurt elbow close to his side.

"Auntie Lum's gonna go, baby," she said.

The little boy looked up. "Why?"

"Come here, honey." Lum hugged him as he stood between her legs. "Auntie Lum sometimes goes to Aunt Ethel and Uncle Jimmy and Uncle Walter's house, and it's time for me to go."

"When're you coming back?"

"I'm not sure. But I'll be back." She pulled out her carpetbag, given to her by Granny. Newspaper clippings and postcards lined the bottom. She wrapped the postcards in a piece of cloth from Granny's favorite apron and placed them in her cedar box.

When they arrived at her family farm, Ethel was in the hog pen. She climbed out and went to Al's side of the truck. "What're y'all doing here?"

Lum looked at Al, wondering how to say Margaret kicked her out. She leaned toward Al. "Well, Margaret thought it would be a good time for me to come help you out."

Fists on her waist, Ethel squinted in the twilight. "Ain't time for you to come back."

"Please, Margaret doesn't . . ."

Al interrupted, saying, "We don't want to upset the apple cart. I'm sure someone else can take her."

"Who?" Lum asked. Why was he acting as if it weren't her he was talking about?

Al shrugged and started up the engine. After a mile, he said, "How about Mrs. Hurston?" Lum had helped the postmistress's mother last year. Al dropped her off at the post office. "Sorry, Lum, but I better get on home. Margie will have supper waiting."

The truck sped away before Lum could find out if Mrs. Hurston needed her.

After she asked Mrs. Hurston about her mother, the postmistress said, "This colored woman's been comin' over every day. Mrs. Scott is expecting. She may need you."

Lum walked cautiously in the dark to the mill owner's house.

Mr. Scott opened the door, saying, "What you doing out this time of night?"

Near tears and hungry, Lum said, "I heard Mrs. Scott may need some assistance."

"Who told you that?"

"Folks talk."

"Who's saying that about my wife?" He blocked the doorway.

"It was Mrs. Hurston. She doesn't mean no harm. She's trying to be helpful. Please don't say anything to her."

"I don't want my baby to be marked, you understand?"

Lum dropped her head. She knew what he meant. She'd heard of babies being marked by something the mother saw when expecting. No one had ever said this about her. At least not that she knew.

"Look," he said. "You can't stay here. You got any place to stay? Family?"

"They don't want me."

"Tell you what. Go get in the car. I'll get you a blanket and take you to the schoolhouse. There's a stove to keep you warm. I'm sure in the light of day you'll figure something out."

Mr. Scott built a fire in the wood stove then hurried home. It took Lum a long time to get to sleep on the hard floor, going over in her mind the fight with Margaret; how Ethel had looked when she said, "Ain't time for you yet"; Mr. Scott saying he didn't want his baby marked; Mrs. Hurston saying they had a colored woman. Then she thought about where she could go. Seemed she had only fallen asleep when the door creaked open to early dawn and Miss Liza Shay was standing over her.

"Miss Carson," the schoolteacher said. "What are you doing here?"

Lum sat up quickly. "I'm sorry. I didn't have any place to go."

"No place?" Liza squatted beside her.

"No. I don't know what to do."

"Oh my," Liza said.

"I'm sorry, I'll go."

"You don't have to, but I don't know how to help you."

"I'll think of something." But what? Apologize to Margaret? Beg Ethel? Go directly to Jimmy, not his wife?

"Take your time. The children will be here soon, but don't feel you have to hurry off."

She didn't want the children to see her like this, so she folded up the blanket. "Would you make sure Mr. Scott gets this?"

"Have you had anything to eat?"

Lum shook her head.

Liza handed her ten cents. "Go to the store and buy yourself a little something."

"That's kind, but I don't know when . . ."

"Pay me back when you can."

With her bag in hand, Lum headed out the door, almost colliding with Raymond, Jimmy's son. His sister was right behind him.

"Hello, Auntie Lum," her nephew said.

"Hi, Raymond, Sally." She looked around. "Where's Junior?"

"He's hepping with them hogs."

Lum remembered working the hogs in late summer. That was something she could do. If she offered to help, Junior wouldn't have to miss school. After getting some bread and apple butter from the store she walked to her family's farm. She begged Ethel to let her come back early, promising to help with the hog killing.

"Well, I reckon you'll be right handy," her sister-in-law said. "I'm sorry about last night, but we have a schedule for you."

Margaret's Crazy Idea

1933

After Dan went back to sleep, Lum sat with her feet propped in front of the coal stove, drying out her shoes and reading about types of whales. She'd never known that whale oil had been used in lanterns, much less that it came from a particular kind of whale. The scene where the men squeezed the whale fat through their fingers, making their hands feel so soft when rubbed against each other, stuck in her mind.

When Liza got home, Lum put *Moby Dick* back on the shelf and headed toward Amy's. A large walnut tree was split down the trunk, probably hit by lightning the night before. Smoke was rising from Amy's chimney. Lum quickened her pace, hoping to see Smiley there, out of jail.

When she knocked, Amy opened the door slightly. "Back so soon?"

"Hello," Lum said. "I wanted to see if you have anything for bad headaches." *And to find out about Smiley*, she thought.

"The kind of headache makes you sick to your stomach?"

"Why, yes. You know the kind that pounds atop your eyebrow?"

Amy narrowed her eyes. "Just the one side of your head?"

Lum nodded.

"Oh, them are bad. For the headache, you can mash up some mountain mint and apply it to your temples. Make yourself a tea with catnip for your upset tummy and lay down awhile." She looked through some small sacks, often smelling before passing to the next one. "Mr. Youngblood was here to buy a bunch of herbs, so we just bagged up everything. I'm sorry I sold him all the feverfew I had."

While Amy looked for the herbs, Lum took a quick look around the cabin for Smiley, but the bed where she'd seen him earlier was made up with a flat quilt, not the pile that he'd been resting his leg on. "I heard talk in town about Smiley Hawkins being in jail. Wasn't he staying here?"

"Oh, we worried something awful about him. The sheriff brought him back from jail, 'cause he didn't do nothing wrong. He's staying at the Reverend and Miss Myrtle's house."

"But what happened? Was Smiley involved in Mr. Snell's accident?"

"He said Mr. Snell got hisself run over."

"How?"

Amy shook her head. "Alls I heard is Smiley was helping Mr. Snell, but he got blamed for it. His aunt was so upset about him being in jail she came here and said Smiley belonged with his family, so off he went." Amy scooped a small pile of herbs into a paper sack and handed it to Lum. "This here's the mountain mint."

After Lum paid for the herbs, she walked to the road and paused. If she turned left, she could go to the Reverend's house and see Smiley. Not only could she find out how he was, but also what had happened to Mr. Snell. She had to decide: home to Margaret, or to Smiley. If she went directly to the farm, she'd be early enough for Margaret to not be mad about her being late, and she and Margaret could prepare a nice supper together. On the other hand, Margaret was so starved for gossip she wouldn't care when Lum got there if she had facts about Snell's accident. She could always tell Margaret about Mr. Snell, and when she asked more questions, Lum could suggest a visit to Smiley. Staying in Margaret's good graces outweighed her curiosity about Smiley. Foolishly, she had forgotten to even ask Amy how Smiley was doing. He couldn't be too bad off if he was able to walk over to his uncle and aunt's house.

By the time she reached the farmhouse, she was exhausted, and the paper sack of herbs was damp where she'd carried it in her sweaty hand. Margaret was in the kitchen nursing Meg.

"How's she feeling today?"

"Little cranky."

"Let me fix up more of that medicine." Lum lit the stove and shook the teakettle to make sure it held water. She looked out the kitchen window at the hogs lying about and thought of Cyrus Snell in the mud under a car. "You'll never guess what happened last night!" Lum exclaimed.

Her cousin looked up. "Did you find out something about Al?"

"No, but get this, Cyrus Snell got trapped under a car Smiley Hawkins was in up High Ford Road." Lum told what she'd heard and how Amy had said "he got hisself run over."

"What does that mean?" Margaret puzzled.

"I don't know. Only one could tell is Smiley."

Margaret pulled Meg's head away and buttoned her dress. "If he done something to Mr. Snell, he wouldn't tell the truth no ways, not after what Al said Cyrus done to him."

"But the sheriff let him out of jail."

Margaret continued, "And what in the world was Mr. Harper doing with a bunch of them? He don't even live around here no more. Tomorrow you go to town early, see what you can find out. I just can't imagine this county without Cyrus Snell telling everybody what to do."

"Don't forget Braxton." *He'd be worse than his father,* she thought.

"Oh, Braxton. Oh, my, Mr. Cock-a-doodle-do!"

They laughed.

Lum didn't tell her that Al had invited Braxton to dinner. Better not. Anything that would make Margaret mad Lum wanted to avoid since she seemed to be in a better mood. Maybe she and Al had had a nice dinner together. "What you thinking for supper?"

Margaret's eyes shone. "I'd just love sauerkraut and potatoes. Why don't you make some of your good biscuits? I churned some fresh butter today."

Just as Lum reached for the dough bowl, Caleb and Al burst in.

"Niggers tried to kill Mr. Snell last night!" Caleb yelled.

"That's not what happened!" Lum spun around.

"Uh-huh. He's in the hospital near dead. Tommy Buck said so."

"It was an accident. Nobody tried to kill him."

"How do you know?" Al said, looking from his son to Lum.

"That's what I heard in town around the Resettlement Off . . ."

Uh-oh, she shouldn't have mentioned that name.

"Who said?"

"Well, folks. They arrested Smiley but let him go 'cause he didn't do nothing wrong. There's even talk it was Smiley saved Mr. Snell's life."

Al snorted. "That'll be the day. Snell beat the tar out of him!"

Margaret said, "You think Smiley tried to get him back?"

"Of course," Al replied.

"No colored person would lay a hand on Cyrus," Lum said. "You know Smiley. You really think he'd kill him?"

Al stared at Lum. "You turning into a nigger lover? How come you taking the side of Smiley against one of our own?"

Lum felt her face burn, indignant that he would talk to her that way. And Cyrus one of her own? He'd been nothing but hateful to her.

Al turned to his son. "Boy, how does Tommy Buck know?"

"His daddy talked to the deputy." Caleb puffed out his chest. "And Mr. Braxton said he'd string up whoever done it."

Lum gasped. "He said that? String him up?" She swung her gaze from Caleb to Al. "We can't let him do that. Talk to Braxton, Al. Tell him Smiley wouldn't do nothing like that."

"Don't get so excited," Al urged. "Braxton is all talk."

"Coloreds been hanged for no reason. Remember Clyde Jackson when we was young?"

"That kind of stuff don't happen no more, Lum. You know of a single nigger been hung since Clyde? No."

"I don't care. I'm gonna warn him."

"Don't get messed up in this. It ain't none of your concern." Spying the dough bowl, he said, "Biscuits is your business, that's all." Al put his hand on his son's shoulder. "Let's get washed up for supper."

When Caleb and Al left the kitchen, Margaret said, "You're determined to go see that nigra, aren't you? What is it about him?"

"I've known him since I was a young'un. I just don't want nothing bad to happen to him. And he's a good person. He wouldn't kill nobody, not even his worst enemy." She flipped the dough onto a board and pounded it. Smiley was in real danger. She didn't believe for a moment that lynching had stopped. Just because it hadn't happened to anyone they knew for a long time didn't mean a hothead like Braxton wouldn't carry out his threat. She slapped and kneaded the dough in hopes of driving out the image of Clyde's swinging legs in holey pants.

1910

One day, just as the family was sitting down for supper, Tommy Lee ran in shouting, "A nigger got hung! Can we go see 'im?"

Daddy jumped up from the table's long bench. "Where? Who?"

"Some nigger called Clyde."

"Clyde Jackson? He's one of them Snell sharecroppers."

Lum hadn't heard of people being hung. She thought people went to jail, but she supposed if the crime were bad enough, they'd be hung. But wouldn't that happen in Richmond or Petersburg? Everyone was afraid of Petersburg. When the boys did something wrong, Daddy would say if they didn't straighten up, they'd end up in Petersburg.

"Let's go see," Guthrie said.

"He's in that clearing halfway up High Ford Road," Tommy Lee said.

All the boys headed for the door. "Come on, Lum," Jimmy said.

She didn't know if she wanted to see a hanged man, but she was curious.

"Not me," Granny said. "I oncet saw a colored woman hanging from a bridge. Most horrible thing I ever saw. You don't want to go, Lum."

"Lum," called Guthrie. "Don't be so chicken."

She wavered for a minute, then decided to follow Daddy and the boys. Their father knew a shortcut through the woods. He carried a lantern and they all followed. Before long they heard voices and a lot of laughter.

Folks were standing around the lynched man laughing. Some were cutting off fingers or toes. Others cut scraps of his clothing. A hefty man held up a severed thumb as if he'd won first prize at the county fair. Clyde's pink swollen tongue protruded, his eyes open in surprise. When Guthrie ran toward Clyde, her father called him back.

"Boys," he said, "I don't want nothing of his in my house."

Jugs of moonshine were passed around the crowd, and three men approached the hanged man. When they pulled down his pants, Lum saw a long knife gleam under its owner's torch.

Daddy pulled her away, his hand over her eyes. "Let's go. We've seen enough."

She wanted his hand to take away what she'd already seen. Lum wished Granny had made her stay home, because she couldn't forget the sight. She held her Daddy's rough hand all the way home. Daddy was quiet, but the boys were excited, and they chattered as they made their way through the dark woods.

For months afterward, her brothers would mimic Clyde, heads to one side, sticking out their tongues, and holding up three fingers. Lum would run away, sobbing, as they hooted.

1933

After making biscuits, Lum had used some of the dough to make blackberry cobbler with canned berries that Caleb had picked in late summer, and served it topped with fresh cream.

"Umm." Al smacked his lips. "Nothing like blackberries!" He scraped the bowl clean, pushed back from the table, and announced that he was going out.

"Oh, honey, not tonight." Margaret grabbed his shirttail.

"Let me go, woman," he teased.

"Where you going?" She dropped her hand to her lap and covered it with the other one as if to prevent it from springing up again.

"Roadhouse." He looked away.

"Why you have to go there every night?"

"That's where I get news about what's going on. Ain't you curious?"

"Yeah, I am. Take me with you."

"That's no place for you." Al stood. "Stay here with the children."

"Lum can take care of 'em, can't you?" She turned to Lum.

Concentrating on removing seeds imbedded in her teeth with her tongue, Lum nodded, but she was planning to slip out to Smiley's. She hoped Al would quash Margaret's request. Of course he would. Time to clear the table and avoid being brought into this old argument. She stacked some dishes and headed for the sink.

"Margaret, nobody brings their wife. It's just not right for a wife and mother."

"I bet there's floozies there."

Al rested his hands on the back of his chair. "No floozies, just men."

Margaret whined, "You didn't use to go out all the time."

"I have to find out about the Scenic. They want the farm, Margaret!"

In a small voice she responded, "I know. But don't stay out too late."

After Al left, Margaret joined Lum at the sink. "What if you went to the roadhouse? Then you could tell me what goes on there."

"Me?!" Lum jerked her hands out of the soapy water.

"Why not?" Margaret leaned closer.

"He'll see me." Lum's left eye twitched at the thought of entering an unfamiliar place.

"You could put on a disguise so nobody recognizes you."

"What kind of disguise?"

"You could dress like a man. No one would ask why you were in the roadhouse."

"Are you off your rocker?" Her days of wanting to wear boys' clothes were over. Granny had pushed that desire right out of her.

"Lummy," she pleaded, "I need to know what he's doing."

"He just told you. He's talking to the other men about that road." Lum turned back to scrubbing the cobbler pan. "And I bet he'll find out about Cyrus getting run over." But she would find out first if she could just go to Smiley.

"You'll just make sure what he's really doing."

"That's the craziest thing you ever thought up. And you came up with some doozies when you were little. Remember when you wanted to teach your dolls to swim, then got upset when they all got swept downstream?"

"I was five years old!"

"And what do you think will happen when Al sees me—in disguise, no less? He'll know you don't trust him." Her wide fingernails scraped stuck-on dough from the pan.

"He wouldn't know it was you if you wore a hat and big coat."

"No." Lum plunged her hands in hot water and felt around for the cloth. "Don't ask me again, because I won't do it." She hardly ever said "no" to one of her relatives, and it felt good to do so.

Unexpected Visits

1933

Lum didn't doubt Braxton would carry out his threat if he thought Smiley had tried to kill his father. But Al had invited Braxton to dinner. She didn't know how she could stand to feed him or even sit at the same table. Even now, she could recreate the feeling of him pushing her with both palms flat against her breasts. Did he think of it when he saw her?

Her lantern only cast a small circle of light, so she swung it from side to side. When she had lit the lamp, she'd smelled it, remembering the Pequod's mission, but it didn't smell fishy. Of course, whale oil was no longer used for lighting oil. Suddenly, a large, pointy nose scurried in front of her. She gasped. An opossum glowed in the light then just as suddenly disappeared.

Although she knew where the Reverend and his wife lived, she had never been there. When she saw the gate, she rushed forward. She realized this was the second time today she'd gone to a colored person's house. She knocked and the door was opened by Smiley's aunt.

"Hello, I'm looking for Smiley."

"Yes, ma'am, he's in the barn. Would you like me to go fetch him?" Myrtle started down the ramp.

Lum blurted, "I can go out there." She'd rather his aunt not hear what she had to say. "You stay here and I'll go."

"Yes, ma'am." Myrtle turned and disappeared into the house.

A faint glow escaped through the slats of the old tobacco barn. When she entered, it smelled musty, but the barn floor was the cleanest she'd ever seen. Smiley was in a rattan wheelchair beside a young woman who was sitting on a pile of feed bags.

"Smiley!" Lum rushed forward. "What happened last night?"

"Miz Lum!" He sounded as surprised to see her as she was to see him in a wheelchair.

"But I didn't know you were crippled. I thought Amy was just keeping you still so your knee could heal."

He looked like he'd been hit by her words. "I was walking right before you got here, wasn't I, Hilda?"

Hilda nodded. "I better get on home."

"Don't go yet. Can you go into my room and bring me that cigar box by my bed?"

"Yeah, but it's getting late. I have to get the boys to bed."

After Hilda left, Smiley asked, "Miz Lum?"

"I've come to warn you, Smiley. I heard Braxton Snell is making threats against you. Watch out for him. Maybe go somewhere he won't know about."

"The sheriff already told me and he said he'd talk to Mr. Braxton. I'm just praying Mr. Snell gets better so he can tell everybody what really happened."

"What did happen up there?"

"Mr. Harper brung me this here chair 'cause he felt bad about me getting beat up, and I asked if he'd take me up to the Honey Man's. See, folks can't get no honey because I can't get around good. We was coming down the mountain and it was raining something awful and Mr. Harper can't see through the storm and we ran off the road and got stuck. The Honey Man and his boys was helping us push the car. Well, here comes Mr. Snell and he tries to tell us what to do and gets in the car, one foot in and one foot out to steer while them boys push. I was in the backseat all the time. Somehow the car slipped down the slope and Mr. Snell got caught up under the car. "

"My goodness." Lum gasped.

"The boys were rocking the car with me still in it to get him from under the wheel. I was about to get sick so I crawled out of the back and told them to dig a trench to roll him into while some'a them pick up the car on that side. It worked!"

"That was good thinking."

"If I wanted to get back at him, don't you see that would have been the perfect time?"

She nodded. "I heard you was in jail."

"So they put Mr. Snell in his own car and I got in with Mr. Harper and we was hurrying to take him to the hospital. The sheriff stops us 'cause we're in Mr. Snell's car and he looks half-dead. He takes me and Mr. Harper to the sheriff's and I end up in a cold cell most the night. The sheriff takes Mr. Snell to the hospital and then Mr. Harper shows him where his car is stuck. They believed Mr. Harper, and the sheriff took me back to Amy's. But Aunt Myrtle wanted me back home."

"But still, Braxton could bring a gang of men here."

"I'll leave that in the Lord's hands. Don't you worry about ol' Smiley." He fingered his top lip.

Lum had known him long enough to tell that he didn't seem quite so sure. She could hear Dessa saying, "Keep an eye on my boy, please, ma'am?" How could she do that now?

"You need to take this seriously, Smiley. Don't think it can't happen."

"The sheriff says he can calm down Mr. Braxton."

Lum knew all too well how white men stuck together. *But still, the fact that the sheriff found it necessary to warn him—what did that mean? That it was a reason to worry, or that the sheriff would keep Braxton from doing anything?* Her thoughts were interrupted by Hilda bringing the box. Lum looked away while Smiley kissed Hilda goodbye.

"Miz Lum, I got new cards. You ever seen a colored albino?"

"No, just white ones." She wondered how an albino could be colored.

He pulled three cards from the box. In the first one, a young female albino with a broad nose and thick lips had a snake that must be ten feet long wrapped around her bare shoulders. "Oh, my!" Lum exclaimed.

"Wait'll you see this one." Smiley held out a card picturing a handsome man in an elaborate East Indian costume with a headless female twin, wearing pantaloons and a skirt, emerging from his stomach. "That's Laloo, the Hindoo." Smiley pointed.

"These are so different," Lum exclaimed.

"What about this?" Smiley handed her the last one. Fine hair six inches long covered the face of a pug-nosed man. "Lionel the Lion-Faced

Man," she read. How exciting—three new cards just in time for the Fat Lady's new sideshow.

A cold wind in Lum's room took advantage of cracks around the window and door. Once inside, Lum grabbed a shawl and draped it around her shoulders, then stretched out across the yellowing quilt, glad she had seen Smiley. After the shock of him in a wheelchair, she felt better knowing that he was starting to walk. And he was less worried about Braxton than she was. Or was Smiley just more hopeful that Mr. Snell would survive to tell how Smiley helped?

Now she had to fret about another one of Margaret's crazy schemes. She always came up with odd ideas. One time Margaret sewed little trousers for the dolls so they could join the Civil War, carrying clothespins for rifles. Aha! So that was where she got the idea of Lum dressing like a man.

Lum pulled the new cards out of her dress pocket. Laloo, Lionel, and the Albino. What would she name her? Albina? That was a pretty name. Lum rolled off the bed and reached for the valise by her bed. She searched for a card with a tattooed man. Usually she didn't like the cards with folks who made themselves into freaks with things like tattoos. Nor did she care for midgets. She had a card with a whole family of midgets. If a midget never left his family he'd never know he was different. Being different than those who love you was what set you apart.

One card pictured a tall man wearing only a loincloth. His entire body was decorated with fantastical beasts, faces, swirling lines, and words. She'd call him Queequeg. No. Quigley. She picked up the card with the Fat Lady sitting on a trunk, gigantic ankles showing below a skirt. Behind her was a red banner advertising "Fraulein Mittilein, the Heaviest Woman Alive." The back of the card stated that she loved to eat and hoped to eventually weigh one thousand pounds.

When she got off the train, the Fat Lady looked around, not knowing who would be there to take her to the carnival. She saw men with beards, small children, ladies who were a little larger than normal, but no one looked like a sideshow person or any type of carny. Finally her eyes rested on a man, shirtsleeves rolled up to the elbows, with patterns of lions and tigers running down his forearms. When she felt those eyes traveling up her body, she waved, hoping he was there to take her to the carnival. He lifted ink-darkened fingers in response, and they pushed through the other passengers toward each other.

Lum, holding one card in her left hand and another in her right, wagged the two cards at each other as Quigley, the Tattooed Man, and Fraulein Mittilein shook hands, hers plump with hidden bones, his callused and black-inked. They hurried off, knowing they shouldn't let ordinary people see them for free. Soon Fraulein would meet the Bearded Lady, Lionel, Laloo the Hindoo, and Albina. Violet and Daisy and the Pin Heads and Lobster Boy were all back with Mr. Day's Seven Special Delights. "Don't worry, Daisy and Violet, I won't abandon you," Lum whispered to the postcard with the twins standing, joined at an angle, and playing saxophones. What if one of the special people ran a sideshow instead of some man with black whiskers and a top hat? With the Fat Lady going to Pittsburgh, Lum could create a whole new world.

Branches scratched against the window when the wind blew stronger, then seemed to rap on it. She jumped. Someone was out there, looking in at her. Lum saw Kenny's face, framed by a pair of palms, his nose pressed against the glass. She pointed toward the door. As soon as his face was gone, she put the cards in the valise and snapped it shut before she opened her door.

"Where's Al?" Kenny asked. "His truck's gone."

"He's at that roadhouse." Lum drew the door wider.

"Can I come in? It's cold." His thermal-clad arms wrapped around his thin frame.

"Not much warmer in here." Lum stepped back so he could enter.

"I don't know where to go. The Knob ain't safe no more." His voice shook.

"What happened?"

He settled into the chair next to her bed, shivering. She was afraid he'd catch cold. She arranged the shawl around his shoulders, fingers trembling lest he shrink from her touch. She sat on the edge of the bed, their knees just inches apart.

He pulled the shawl tighter. "Me 'n Granny were having some

squirrel stew when Abe and Jeremiah Collins came up with long rifles and started yelling for me to come out. When I did, they said I was a traitor for trying to run 'em out of their homes. All because I was going around with Mr. Shapiro. He was offering folks lots of money for their houses, but not a one of 'em took his offer. So Mr. Shapiro said for me to go myself to talk to folks. Everybody already knew about the road and said 'no' before I could even tell 'em anything. News travels on air around the Knob. When I got to my sister's house she wouldn't even come to the door. Her little girl said her mama didn't have no brothers and 'don't come back.'" His voice cracked.

"Oh." Lum remembered that Kenny had been involved in drowning his sister's husband.

"After that, I went on home. I don't know why I let Mr. Shapiro talk me into getting folks to sell their homes. I thought it would be better than road work, but they think I'm turning on 'em." His fingers protruded through open spaces in the crocheted shawl, locked together. "You think that's what I'm doing?"

"No. What if someone wanted to sell their house? They'd be glad you told them."

Shaking his head, Kenny continued, "You know how the farmers were in that meeting? My people were worse. It was like I asked for their baby, their cow, and their rifles. Like it's all *my* fault." Suddenly he sat up straight. "Shh, what's that noise?"

Lum listened. Nothing. "Just some leaves, I think."

"Maybe we should dim the light," he whispered.

She turned the lantern key so the flame went down, but not all the way.

He said softly, "We've been on the Knob since before Virginia was even a state."

"But what's up there?" Lum puzzled. "Isn't it hard to grow anything so high up?"

"Folks hunt and gather sang and walnuts to sell, and make moonshine. We know them woods like our own home." His voice rose an octave. "Why'd I try to get 'em to leave?"

"You were offered a job, that's all. They'll forgive you."

"No." He hung his head. Lum wanted to stroke the shiny hair.

"Turning on your own ain't right. Ever since I got back from jail, it's been hard. I miss my daddy and Early. And the other fellas. I became a man in prison. Them Collinses don't hate me for killing a man, but they hate me now, and they're gonna get me. Granny was so upset, I decided to leave so nothing bad would happen to her. I can't go back."

"Sounds like you don't want to work for Mr. Shapiro no more."

"It ain't that easy. If I hadn't never been to prison I would'a never left the Knob. But the men in prison were always talking about ways to get money. That's what they talked about night and day. Money, money, money, and how to get it. I wanted an honest life, to work and make my own money. I thought if I got out, I'd never go back; now I see how some men keep ending up in jail, 'cause they forgot how to live free." He stretched. "All I thought about was getting out. Now I'm out, but I'm not free. I wish I could get me my own place to live. More than anything, that's what I'd like." Kenny gazed up at her. "You're so easy to talk to. I'm sorry to rattle on like a cornered snake."

Lum could have listened to him all night. Arguing with himself, trying to figure out what he wanted. Maybe if she could talk to someone like that, she could figure herself out.

"I was hoping Al was here so I could tell him I'm on his side. I'm indebted to him for helping me when nobody else would."

"Let's not disturb Margaret. You just stay here with me 'til Al gets home."

"I don't want to bother you more'n I already have."

"You're no bother." She pulled the quilt up to her chest but couldn't stop trembling.

"What was you doing when I come up?"

"Oh, just thinking." She hoped he hadn't seen the cards.

Feet Warming

1933

The last thing Lum remembered was listening to Kenny, and struggling to stay awake. His life seemed like it had been ideal before the incident with the brother-in-law. Lum pulled the quilt closer, covering her chilled backside. She felt something under her rump. Something long and bumpy. Now she saw Kenny's chin slumped to his chest, and she realized it was his feet tucked under her. She felt warmth spreading down her hips to between her legs. Slowly she reached out, tenderly touching his chilly ankles. When had he slipped off his boots and put the stockinged feet on her bed? Had they slept like that all night?

She remembered, when she was ten years old, sleeping with an infant squirrel she'd named Spunky. It had fallen out of a tree and she'd fed it with a doll bottle, but her daddy and grandmother kept telling her to let it go and be a squirrel. She refused because it was the only living thing that belonged to her. One night she must have rolled over on Spunky, because when she woke up his stiff corpse was sandwiched between her waist and elbow. She wished she could have turned back time and let Spunky be with the other squirrels. Afterwards, whenever she wanted a kitten or puppy, Granny would say, "Remember what you did to Spunky. You love animals too much."

She hated to disturb Kenny, but surely it was time to get up and start breakfast. Or was it that she was enjoying warming his feet? Or the warmth between her legs like when she touched herself? If only she could seal in the tingling sensation by crossing her legs. She imagined Ishmael and Queequeg keeping each other warm when they shared a bed. Slowly, she rolled away from the long feet.

"What?" Kenny jerked. "Who's there?"

"It's all right, you just fell asleep." Lum smoothed her dress. She'd never changed into her night clothes.

"It's morning?"

"Yes." She hesitated, wanting to stay with him, to not break the spell, but not wanting Margaret to see him. "I reckon we both fell asleep, not meaning to." She slowly lowered her feet to the cold floor and stood with the bed between them.

"Sorry. I thought I'd hear Al coming home."

"It's fine." Lum looked down. "Well, I'm gonna get some eggs." She wanted him to stay for breakfast, but how could she explain to Al and Margaret? She should at least offer food. "You want something to eat?"

"No. I gotta get going." Kenny stood, facing the door.

"But didn't you need to talk to Al? We could pretend you just got here."

"I'll come back later, maybe when he's out to the pasture, so we can talk. In the meantime, tell him what I said about being on his side. I better head for the highway, try to catch Mr. Shapiro before he gets to the Knob. No telling what them Collinses got planned for *him*."

They both hurried out the door and off the porch. Then, without saying good-bye, they walked in opposite directions. At least he wouldn't have to walk through the house. No one would know he'd been there. She hoped he wouldn't leave tracks in the frost. Were she and Kenny now friends? She always had family, no friends. How about Dan? Was he a friend? He'd acted like it yesterday. Now she looked forward to going to his house again. She decided to make a nice breakfast and then leave for town and hope Margaret wouldn't stop her.

After washing the breakfast dishes, Lum tied a wool scarf under her chin.

"Where you off to?" Margaret asked.

"Why, to Dan Shay's, of course." She'd hoped Margaret had forgotten about what she'd said yesterday.

"You can't go today." Margaret's voice rose. "Braxton Snell's coming for supper tonight. We gotta get started cleaning. I want to wash the windows and curtains and sweep and mop and dust. Ain't you even pondered what we'd serve?"

"I thought he might not come 'cause of his daddy being laid up in the hospital."

"Oh, I didn't think of that." Margaret drummed fingers against her closed mouth. "What if we clean up a storm and cook a feast fit for a king, and he doesn't come?"

"Then we'll have a clean house. And lots of food." Lum wished he wouldn't come. She was hoping to read more of *Moby Dick* today. She swallowed. "I'll come back early."

"But I cain't do it all. You know how Meg is. If I start sweeping, she'll get to sneezing and crying and I'll have to take care of her."

Lum suppressed a laugh, remembering Dan saying Margaret had that baby and could take care of it herself. Margaret *did* act like she was the only woman to ever have a baby and have to clean and cook. She didn't want to have to repeat what Dan said about the school closing if Lum didn't take care of him. Margaret would have a fit. She might even stop talking again. How could Lum convince Margaret that she had to go to town today?

"How about I make a special cake for tonight? Remember how much Al liked that chocolate cake with cherries between the layers?"

Margaret nodded. "He said he hoped you'd make it again."

"What if I go to Mr. Shay's, make sure he gets some dinner, then go get some canned cherries and cocoa powder down at the store? When I get back, we'll clean up lickety split." She imagined the rich aroma of chocolate cake seeping from the oven and then the cake, covered with whipped cream, as a centerpiece to the meal. She'd also fry some chicken, make mashed potatoes and gravy. Whatever Al liked, she'd make, so he would be proud to serve a meal to the man who might soon be the richest in town. She'd better hurry if she was going to get out the door while Margaret was thinking about a cake. If she planned right she'd be able to get everything done and make everyone happy, maybe even herself.

"That'd be all right, I reckon," Margaret said slowly. "But don't dilly-dally. Come on back. We want everything to be just right."

Dan Does Some Business

1933

How would she tell Dan she'd have to leave early, Lum wondered. Mentioning Braxton Snell was not a good idea, not after the coughing fit that had put Dan back in bed. At least if he slept, she could read some. But she better get that idea out of her head. No *Moby Dick* today if she had to leave early. Ishmael and them would have to keep on sailing without her. Maybe Dan would offer again to let her borrow it.

The shawl Kenny had slept with was wrapped around her head to keep her ears warm against the cold wind as she entered Granite Falls. She held it over her nose and smelled his man's scent. Her shoes weren't really made for a lot of walking, and her feet felt like they were breaking the ice on a washbasin with every step. When she crossed the town square, she noticed church ladies going into the First Baptist Church, many of them carrying piles of clothes. They had swap meets from time to time. She'd bought the pair of shoes she was wearing now from the church sale, and they'd lasted about ten years. If she could gather up some clothes from Margaret, she'd have something to trade and maybe get new shoes. She walked toward the church, aiming for a pair of gray-haired church members, one tall, one short.

"Hello," she called, trying for a lilt to her deep voice.

"Morning," sang out the short woman.

"Are you getting ready for a swap meet?"

"It don't start 'til tomorrow," the tall one snapped.

Lum asked, "Can we bring clothes in the morning?"

"If you get here early enough," the short one said. "We open at seven

155

with coffee and baked goods. We're expecting a big turnout with all the new men in town." Pausing to look up and down Lum's body, she continued, "Bring men's clothes if you have any."

"I'll see you tomorrow, then." Lum hoped she could gather some men's clothing to trade. Al's would probably be too worn to resell, though. Maybe Dan had some.

Dan and Liza's yard was getting browner every day. When she knocked on the front door, she heard male voices. Suddenly, the door was opened by Mr. Harper. She was startled to see him after hearing about his adventure. He must have gotten his car off the mountain. He was wearing a black suit and his starched white sleeves protruded from the suit jacket. Shiny cufflinks with a blue gemstone glinted when he held out his hand.

"Miss Columbia Carson," he boomed.

She shook his hand briskly before realizing he was just holding her hand like a limp washrag. She hated when a man took her hand that way.

"How do you do, Mr. Harper?" She loosened her grip.

"Come on in." Mr. Harper beckoned. "Mr. Shay's in the kitchen."

"Morning," she sang out when she saw Dan sitting at the table with official-looking papers spread all over.

"Well, well, well, Columbia, good morning." Dan had a gleam in his eye. He wore a white shirt that sagged on his thin frame, dress pants, and leather shoes. He held a piece of paper at arm's length, squinting at a long column of numbers. Two cups half-full of light brown coffee sat amidst the papers.

She wouldn't say anything about him putting milk in his coffee. He wouldn't want the lawyer to see him "being babied." She watched while Dan would sign something, then Mr. Harper would slide another sheet toward him and wait while Dan read and signed that one.

As Mr. Harper stretched his arm, revealing the cufflinks, Lum remembered Smiley saying he had sold Lum's cufflinks. They had been given to her great-grandfather in honor of his work with the Agriculture Department before the Civil War. She hated selling them, but it was the only way she could get money. She hadn't known Liza would be giving her a few coins every day. Smiley sold the cufflinks for ten dollars. That was the most money she'd ever had at one time. *I could take a train trip if I wanted to,* she thought.

"That's it for the one on Adams." Mr. Harper straightened the stack of papers into a neat pile. "Let's start on Franklin."

Unsure of what to do, Lum decided to look in the icebox to see if any of her onion soup was still there. Glass jars holding onion soup and what looked like a new batch of chicken soup were lined up in the icebox. Liza obviously was determined for her father to have chicken broth every day. She wiped off the icebox, the counter, the stove, and finally, the sink. Dan and Mr. Harper were still pushing papers around. What in the world was that all about?

"You hiring folks to get the houses ready?" Mr. Harper gathered up papers.

"Have to." Dan coughed lightly into his closed fist. "The Adams house is in good shape, so we can start renting it out once it's painted. I'll want a housekeeper and cook and someone to keep up the yards. One man can take care of both grounds, but I'll need two women for each one."

Mr. Harper straightened the papers by stacking them and tapping the stacks on the table. "Lots of these men are going down to the road-house after work and they've started cooking a little something for 'em down there."

"If I can provide three good meals a day, I won't lack for roomers."

Lum stopped scrubbing the sink, trying to not be obvious about listening. Her hand was shaking when she resumed wiping. Dan needed a cook. More than one. Would he think of her?

"If there's a need, there's always a business to step in," Mr. Harper proclaimed.

"That's what I aim to do," Dan said. "Before long I reckon more folks will be coming in. Some to work on the road, others will open up businesses, and people driving through, of course. I'll set up Adams as a rooming house for road workers, then when they move on, it'll be for new residents. The Franklin house will be the inn. Beat those Snell bastards at their own game." He snorted. "Trying to get in cahoots with the Highway Commission—they can't stop me fixing up some old houses."

"Shame about Cyrus, though." Mr. Harper looked at the stack of papers.

"Yeah." Dan nodded.

Lum cleared her throat. "Mr. Harper?"

"Yes?"

"I saw Smiley last night. He told me what happened."

He looked surprised. "He did?"

"Yes, sir. And he said something . . . you felt bad about him getting beat up."

Mr. Harper nodded. "I have to admit it *was* my fault. I was handling an estate sale for Cyrus's wife's family. I thought it would be an opportunity for Smiley to make some money and get rid of some of that furniture piled up in his house. He was heading to the sale when Cyrus saw him and whacked him a good one across the knees, and now he can't walk. I brought him a wheelchair and that's when he asked me to carry him up to the Honey Man. It's a big mess and it's all my fault. Me and the Honey Man's boys were trying to get my car out of the mud. Cyrus was jeering at us, saying we didn't know what we were doing, and when he tried to help he got caught under my car. We were jostling the car to get it off him, but Smiley figured out how to get him out. It was hell getting him out'a jail. I was so worried I'd have to get him cleared of an attempted murder charge."

"But can't folks testify that he was trying to help?" Dan asked.

"Not Negroes, not if Cyrus doesn't make it. If he does, Smiley won't have anything to worry about. I convinced the sheriff to let him go once he saw my car up the mountain."

Nothing to worry about, Lum thought. *Tell that to a man who can't walk.* "Last night when I seen him he said Hilda was helping him walk."

"Well, I hope he recovers. I'll do whatever I can to help him, but seems like whenever I show up something bad happens to him." Mr. Harper stood up and pushed the papers into a folder. "I better go on to the bank to finalize the sale."

Dan started to rise, but the lawyer put his hand on Dan's shoulder. "I can see myself out." He stepped back and held out his hand. Dan shook it firmly.

"Thanks for coming by the house."

"Didn't want you to have to go out in the cold."

"I'm getting stronger every day," Dan boasted.

"Glad to hear it. Let me know if there's anything else you need." Mr. Harper grabbed a fedora from the back of a chair.

"I reckon I'm set for now. You know any painters, send 'em my way."

"Will do." He strode to the front door, the sheaf of papers tucked under his arm.

When Lum heard it close firmly behind him, she stopped scrubbing. She looked at Dan's back. He wasn't wide enough to have anything that would fit her. But if he gave her clothes to swap, she could pick out some for the roadhouse, if she decided to do what Margaret asked. She wanted to ask Dan for some clothes but didn't know how. She was curious about the houses he'd bought, and him needing a cook, but didn't want him to think she was nosy or a gossip. "How you feeling today?"

"Better." He coughed several times into his handkerchief, as if he'd been suppressing it during Mr. Harper's visit. "First day I've gotten dressed in the morning. My mother always said you feel better if you get dressed, but I just haven't had the energy." His eyes twinkled. "I didn't let on I shouldn't be drinking coffee. I just had enough to be companionable. Knew you'd fuss if I started hacking blood again."

"So you do listen to me." He was in a good mood. Maybe she could broach the subject. "You go to the Baptist Church, don't you?"

"Sometimes. You're not gonna start preaching at me, are you?"

"Heavens no, not me. They're having one of their rumble sales . . ."

"Rumble sale? You mean rummage? Or jumble?" Dan teased.

She could feel herself blushing. Did he think she was stupid? "Rummage. Swap meet. Anyway, they need lots of men's clothes for those road workers. I reckon they're trying to get 'em some nice suits so they can come to Sunday services."

"Those church ladies are always doing something." He loosened his collar and set it on the table. "Some good works, but you're right, they always try to get more people in the door."

"I was thinking about asking Al for some clothes, but his are probably all worn out." She wondered if he was going to get the hint. If Margaret insisted she wear a disguise, Lum could find some men's clothes at the sale, and if there were lots of men from other places at the roadhouse, Al would never recognize her. She surprised herself how excited she got just thinking about putting on a pair of trousers. If she found a nice suit she could look like a man who was somebody, not just a mysterious stranger in a heavy overcoat.

"I may have some old suits and dress shirts. I don't reckon I'll need many suits just for church and the occasional stop in the bank." He fingered the collar points and sighed. "My banking days are over. Mr. Harper told me the Waynesboro branch closed and he'd have to go to the main branch in Staunton. They're the ones foreclosed on those houses I bought. So I reckon I'll be a landlord and an innkeeper from here on out."

And he needed cooks. Well, she'd have to figure out something really good to cook for him so he'd think of her. Then she told herself to stop dreaming, her family would never let her go.

The Will

1921

Now that she had more postcards with her special people on them, Lum retired her dolls and Bunny from her dramas. They were lined up on her chest of drawers. Bunny and Amy's cloth doll slumped against each other. The bald doll had a bright red scarf, and at times Lum imagined her as the fortune-teller at the fair where Daisy and Violet worked alongside the Armless Woman and the Snake Woman. She had recently gotten The Strongest Man and Lobster Boy. Sitting cross-legged on her bed, she whispered welcomes to Lobster Boy from the others. He looked ordinary except each hand had not fingers but pinchers, as if the fingers were molded together. His thumb was extraordinarily thick.

"Lum," she heard a male voice say, followed by a knock on her locked door. She slipped her cards under her green counterpane.

"What?" She had at least an hour before Ethel would be calling her to help make supper.

"It's that lawyer," Walter said. "The will."

She unlatched her door. Daddy had been against locks on doors, but she had begged him after the time the boys held her down and lifted up her skirt. She hadn't told anybody what they did, but she told Daddy she wanted to be able to change clothes in private. Granny had backed her up.

Daddy had died suddenly. He was out in the pasture chasing a steer that didn't want to be taken to market and was making a run for it. Whenever Lum saw a cow do this she cheered for the cow. But this time, Daddy's horse came back without him. Jimmy rode Daddy's horse and Walter ran behind him. Daddy was lying outstretched on his back, eyes staring upward. Walter started hitting the horse, but Jimmy told him to stop. "Not the nag's fault! She wouldn'a throwed him."

Dr. Miles came out and pronounced him dead of a heart attack. That was a month ago, and Lum still couldn't believe her daddy was gone. Granny was doing a lot worse since she found out about her son's death. She often refused to eat no matter what Lum brought her. Once she discovered that the old woman couldn't refuse applesauce, that's what Lum served often. Of course, that increased her use of a bedpan.

When Lum entered the living room and saw Granny sitting between Jimmy and Ethel, she was surprised to see her. Mr. Harper was sitting in an armchair, and she and Walter settled into other side chairs. He was the young Mr. Harper. His father had been the only lawyer in Granite Falls until his son joined the practice. When he smiled at her, the corners of his mouth seemed to reach to his ears.

"Now that you all are here, let me start by telling you that I was unable to locate your brother, Guthrie. So we don't know if he is dead or alive. The last sighting was at the Roanoke train station, where he bought a ticket in 1920."

Lum noticed Jimmy and Ethel looking at each other over Granny's bowed head.

"He may have been living in Roanoke up to that time but we couldn't find anyone who could confirm that they knew him. And we don't know where the ticket was for." He looked at some papers on his lap.

"Your father had his will drawn up in 1915 and never updated it. It says the land will go to his sons to divide up equally or farm jointly. That means, since there are only two of you that we know are alive, that you two can continue to run the farm together—or, if you want to split it up, I can have a survey done and we'll figure out the best way to split it in two."

Jimmy and Walter looked at each other. Walter shrugged and Jimmy shrugged back.

"You don't have to decide right away. Talk it over." Mr. Harper put a finger under his stiff collar. *He must have dressed up for this visit*, Lum thought. She waited to hear what her father had left to her. She had wondered, even though Jimmy and Walter never mentioned her when they talked about the farm.

"Well, when you need me, drop by the office," Mr. Harper said, standing.

"Wait." Lum's voice trembled. "Isn't there anything . . . ?"

His face softened. "For you?"

She nodded and the room was silent.

"I'm sorry. It only mentions the farm. It'll be up to you all to sort out all the other belongings."

"The house? If they divide up the land, who gets the house?"

"That's what your brothers will have to work out between them."

Granny shifted on the sofa and grunted, waving her left arm.

"Paper?" Lum asked. "Please wait, Mr. Harper, Granny has something to say." She headed to Daddy's room, where the paper was kept, and then returned with a sheet and a pen.

Granny wrote "my will" in a shaky hand and Lum passed it to the lawyer.

He said, "I'll look for it, Mrs. Carson."

Two days later, Lum was feeding the chickens when she saw Mr. Harper's car pull up to the house. She walked toward him and he waved. Once again, she noticed his upturned lips.

"I found your grandmother's will," he called out.

"What do you think she wants with it?" Lum asked.

"No telling. You may want to help me interpret."

"All right," she said, glad to be included.

This time Granny didn't get out of bed. Mr. Harper pulled a chair under the lamp. Lum settled in next to Granny so she could watch her write.

Mr. Harper spoke slowly. "I had to search Father's old files, but I found a will that was made jointly between you and your late husband, Mrs. Carson."

Granny gestured with her left hand and it looked like she wanted him to continue.

"Since it's a joint will, it controls your part of the estate, too."

"But she's not dead," Lum said.

"Of course not, so let me explain." Mr. Harper ran his hand through his thinning hair. Even when he was serious those corners of his mouth tipped upward. He spoke to Lum. "Now, your grandfather's will provided for his son, your father . . ."

Granny hit the quilt with her palm, and when he looked at her, she pointed to her chest.

"Sorry, ma'am." He looked in Granny's direction. "Your husband's will left the farm to his only son. Your only son," he corrected. "It appears that he left you the house and belongings for the rest of your life, then it becomes part of the farm."

Granny wrote: "Can I change?"

"Well." He didn't look up. "I don't know if we can change this will since it's already been executed."

Lum swallowed hard. Was Granny going to leave the house to her? She'd be stuck with Ethel then. Or, Or, she could kick them out and since they had the farm, she could live by herself and Jimmy and Walter would have to build another house for themselves. Granny was going to take care of her after all the times Granny told her to help out family. Granny herself had been raised by her aunt, who never married and took care of the children. But Aunt Harriet had always lived with Granny's family. At least she'd had a permanent home. Or had she? Lum tried to remember. Seems like she'd heard that one of Granny's sisters had made Aunt Harriet leave after her own mother died. She wanted to ask Granny, but it was hard to have a long conversation when the old woman had to write with her left hand.

Granny was writing now. When she'd finished, Lum read: "Belongings to Lum."

Lum thought, *She doesn't want to leave me the house. Why not? Or would she have if Mr. Harper hadn't said it couldn't be changed?*

"Mr. Harper," Lum asked, "Does it say the house *and belongings* return to the farm?"

"Hmmm." He ran his finger down the piece of yellowed paper. "'Upon Mrs. Carson's death, the house shall become part of the farm and will be distributed in accordance thereof.'" He tapped his front tooth with a pen. "Mrs. Carson, within the terms of the will, you may leave any or all of the belongings to whomever you want."

Granny pointed to Lum.

"Yes, ma'am. I'll draft a codicil to the will specifying that all the household furnishings and your personal goods will belong to Lum upon your death."

All the furniture, anything valuable, would be Lum's, and she could do whatever she wanted with them. "Make sure it says Columbia Carson, that's my real name."

"Certainly, Miss Columbia. I'll bring it back next week for you to sign, Mrs. Carson."

After Mr. Harper left, Granny pointed to a cherry box on her chest of drawers. Lum brought it to the bed and they looked at the jet beads, ruby earrings, gold cufflinks, and assorted rings that women of the family had passed down through the last hundred years. Lum remembered hearing stories of who each piece had belonged to and on what occasion they had received it. Granny wrote, "Sell when you need to."

"Any of it?"

Granny nodded.

Friday Night Supper
1933

"Margaret," Lum called, looking around the empty kitchen. She shifted the ball of clothes tied up in one of Dan's tablecloths. It took her a minute to realize what was different. The flour sack curtains were down and sunlight was streaming in through vinegar-streaked windowpanes. So Margaret *had* been cleaning.

"You're back!" Margaret appeared, red hair peeking out of a scarf, dust rag in hand.

"Meg sleeping?"

"Yeah, she took to that catnip tea you brung her."

"Good. I got the chocolate and cherries, and guess what else? I have an idea."

Margaret smiled quizzically. "About what?"

"You know your idea about me going to the roadhouse?"

Her smile widened. "You'll do it?"

Lum nodded toward the bundle of clothes under her arm.

"You found something to wear?"

"Not yet, but I'm taking Dan Shay's clothes to the church swap meet and get me some nice men's clothes. I heard lots of road workers eat at the roadhouse, so nobody'll notice a stranger."

Margaret raised pale eyebrows. "You told Dan about you going to the roadhouse?"

"No!" Lum felt herself blush just thinking about anyone knowing. "Mr. Harper was there, he said it. So what I was thinking was, tomorrow I go to Dan's as usual." She paused. "You need to tell Al some reason I'm not making supper. Like I'm helping with the church sale or something. Then I can get to the roadhouse before Al."

"But," Margaret spurted, "what if he don't go?"

Why did this always happen? Lum wondered. Margaret would ask her to do something, but when Lum agreed, Margaret would come up with objections. "He's been going every night for a month. If I come home and wait for him to leave, I'll have to walk all the way to the other side of town to get there. The whole idea is to show up to eat like the other men. Al won't even notice me 'cause I'll already be there."

Margaret wiped her forehead, smudging it with her dirty cloth. "I'll worry about you. But it'll be worth it to find out what Al's up to."

"Nobody'll bother me." She supposed men didn't worry about where they went and who saw them. "Let me put up the clothes before I start on the cake."

Supper was all cooked, the cake was baked, and their guest hadn't arrived. Al was pacing the kitchen looking first at his pocket watch, then out the window. The sun sank below the horizon, and still no Braxton Snell. Al went to the porch when Margaret told him to stop walking over her clean floor.

The cake had cooled enough to spread cherries between the layers, and Lum was slathering whipped cream on top, when they heard an engine.

"He's here," Caleb called.

"Mind your manners," Margaret whispered to Caleb, and she warned Lum, "Don't say nothing about his daddy's accident or Smiley. And take off your apron."

Lum carried the fried chicken, pork chops, mashed potatoes, milk gravy, string beans, black-eyed peas, stewed tomatoes, and biscuits to the table, hoping Braxton wouldn't pay her much attention. She'd be nice, but only for Margaret and Al. She couldn't forget Braxton's threats against Smiley.

"Uncle Walter!" Caleb ran outside to Braxton's car, where Lum's brother was getting out of the passenger side. Why hadn't Al told her

Walter was coming? What were they up to? Quickly, she added another plate.

Walter and Braxton filed in through the screen door Al was holding open. Walter had the same broad build as Lum. Now that she'd started thinking about wearing a disguise, she found herself sizing up men to see if she could wear their clothes. But she couldn't ask Walter for clothes, because he'd want to know why.

Braxton took off his straw hat and took Margaret's hand. "How do you do?"

"Just fine, Mr. Snell." Margaret took his hat. "How's your Daddy?"

"Still unconscious. Mama's by his side night and day."

"Well, we're all praying."

"Go on and sit down, Braxton." Al gestured toward the table.

"Looks like a feast," he exclaimed, pulling out a chair. Looking at Lum, he said, "I suppose you're responsible for all this."

"Me and Margaret. Ya'll sit. Don't want dinner to get cold." When she passed the fried chicken, she whispered to Caleb, "Just take a wing, so there's plenty for company." He helped himself to a drumstick. Even though Braxton was finally there, Al still kept sneaking peeks at his pocket watch.

After eating in silence for a while, Braxton turned to Al. "You're the luckiest man I know. I've always admired your view of the valley." He sipped some iced tea before continuing, "If I was you, I'd be selling this land for top dollar. You could get you a pretty penny for this place and invest in some other land. Get you just as fine a place on down country. You should take a look around Charlottesville. They got those nice rolling hills. Won't have to worry about the road there."

Al silently sawed a pork chop with his teeth clenched. The mantel clock clicked loudly. Finally, Al said, "You and your daddy selling *your* home place?"

Braxton crossed and uncrossed his legs. "They don't want it. Our house ain't in the road's path."

"What if it was?" Walter, tapping his fork on his plate, stared at him.

"We'd just try to get the best we could out of 'em. That's what we'd do."

"You said the other night that you and your daddy were gonna get top dollar," Al said.

Braxton grinned. "We are, but not for the home place, just up here on the mountain. They're just taking the first half-acre on each side of High Ford Road. We won't lose much tobacco land." He started talking faster. "We're gonna put a lodge up here for the tourists. Folks can hunt or hike or just enjoy the scenery. See, that's why your place is perfect for an overlook."

Lum noticed Walter and Al exchange a glance. Then Walter looked at his lap. Was he, too, looking at *his* watch? Were they planning on going to the roadhouse after dinner? Surely not on the day Braxton came to dinner. She had envisioned a lingering dessert. Of course, her imaginings hadn't included Walter. Why was he here?

"Y'all leave some room for cake," Lum said, trying for levity. "I made something special." When no one said anything, she added, "One of your favorites, Al."

"That's good of you, Lum," Al said, not sounding too excited.

"Chocolate?" Caleb wondered aloud.

"Yes. Good guess."

"I smelled it cooking." He beamed.

Standing to stack plates, Lum noticed her brother and Al both looking at their laps.

BOOM! The night sky lit up. Two smaller explosions followed.

"What the hell!" Braxton's head jerked.

Al's face was bright red. He and Walter seemed to be avoiding looking at each other. Walter's eyes sparkled when he yelled, "What was that?"

"Firecrackers!" Caleb cried out. He jumped up and ran outside.

The three men followed Caleb out the door, excitedly calling out:

"Where is it?"

"Down there!"

"The quarry!"

Margaret and Lum ran outside.

"Margie, go back inside where it's safe," called Al.

Margaret pulled Caleb close to her, but he squirmed away to be with the men.

"Let's go see," Braxton yelled and ran to his car. "Come on," he yelled when Walter and Al hesitated. They looked at each other, and Al ran to the front passenger side. Walter and Caleb jumped into the backseat.

As they sped off, Margaret said, "What you think happened?"

"Don't know. Sounded like the dynamite blasts we used to hear from the quarry back in the old days. But I never heard it after dark."

"They must be blasting for the road."

"Why are the men so agitated if that's all it is?" Lum realized that Braxton was the only one of the men who'd looked startled at the explosion.

Margaret shrugged. "I reckon we'll find out. Let's go cut the cake."

Starting with a thin slice each, then another, Lum and Margaret nibbled, bite by bite, until one-third of the cake was gone. They were both amazed they could still eat after the hearty meal, but they had to do something while they waited.

"Wish they'd get on back. Caleb shouldn't be out this late." Margaret glanced at the door for the twentieth time that night.

"I'm dying to find out what that explosion was." Lum licked cherry juice off her finger.

"You think somebody blew up something?"

"Must have. Wonder what it was." She felt a draft of cold air on her legs. Tomorrow she'll be wearing pants, long pants with pockets and a nice lining. She had ironed enough men's pants to know what they felt like, but not how they felt against her legs. She was tempted to go try on Dan's pants right now. She knew they wouldn't cover her hips, not the way Dan was built, but she just wanted to go feel the fabric in private. "I've got to go to bed."

"Oh, no, Lummy. Can't you stay up a little longer?"

"I'm tired. Don't forget I'm going to that roadhouse tomorrow night. It'll be a long day."

"I reckon you're right. If I don't get some sleep, I won't want to get up to feed Meg."

"Sleep tight." Lum rose to her feet.

"Don't let the bedbugs bite." Margaret carried the cake to the pie safe.

When Lum opened the screen door, she saw lights snaking up the road. She waited between the front door and the entrance to her little room as Braxton's car approached. Caleb jumped out of the backseat and ran to the porch. Seeing her, he exclaimed, "Aunty Lum, you should'a seen it! The earth mover was mangled!" He twisted his arms across his chest. "And a dump truck was all burned up!"

"Oh, my!" she cried. "The machine exploded?"

"Yeah. Bulldozer and a truck and a shack all blown up! Wood and tires and metal all over the place!"

"Where's your daddy and Uncle Walter?" she asked.

"Daddy's still in the car. They took Uncle Walter home. You should'a heard Mr. Snell, he was cussing! Daddy and Uncle Walter were saying bad words, too."

"I bet you're tired as can be." Lum put her hand on his sweaty shoulder.

"No'm. I bet I don't sleep at all tonight. I wish tomorrow weren't gonna be Sairday. I want to tell everybody what I saw."

"Well, come on in and get in bed," Lum urged.

"I want some chocolate cake," he whined.

She hated for him to see how much she and Margaret had eaten. "Maybe a small piece, but then off to bed."

"Yummy!" Caleb skipped toward the kitchen.

Standing at the pie safe, Lum sliced a piece for Caleb and one for Al. Margaret was still at the table. Caleb repeated the story for his step-mother while eating. They heard the car roar away, and Al trudged in.

"Here's some cake, honey," Margaret said.

"Caleb said somebody blew up some road equipment." Lum poured milk for Al and Caleb. "Who would do such a thing?"

Al shrugged. "I'm gonna need something stronger than milk."

"Oh, honey," Margaret complained. "Not tonight."

"Don't fret, I ain't going out." When he pulled a flask from his pocket, Lum noticed his watch fob.

Trying to sound casual, Lum asked, "Why didn't you tell us Walter was coming?"

"What difference does it make?" Al glared. "We had plenty of food."

"But we had to add a chair and plate at the last minute. I just don't see why you didn't tell us so we could set the table properly."

"Lum, sometimes you get my goat! After the night I've had, you're nagging me about putting another damn plate on the table."

Margaret whispered, "Hush up, Lum. It's not important."

Her worried eyes made Lum pause. Lum didn't want Al to take out his anger on his wife. But Al and Walter had been staring at their watches the very instant the explosion happened.

"You're right, it's not important."

"Damn right. Thought you'd be glad to see your brother." He stabbed a piece of cake.

"I was. It was nice of you to invite him." Still, she puzzled over why he and Walter kept looking at their watches, but was hesitant to ask him. "Tell us more about what y'all saw."

Al licked whipped cream from the back of his fork, his tongue ridged between the tines. "Somebody set off dynamite where they keep the road equipment."

"Why?"

Al shrugged again. "Who knows? Braxton was fussing like I know who done it. Finally, I told him to get the hell off my back!" He jabbed a cherry so hard it smashed.

"The sheriff said he's gonna find out who done it!" Caleb shouted.

"Hush," Al said. "All of you, don't say nothing about the explosion. You hear, Lum?"

"Why?" She crossed her arms. Who did he think he was talking to? "Everybody heard it, I'm sure."

"It's just something that happened. I don't want you going around town yapping about it. You, either, Caleb."

"But I want to tell the other boys. Bet none of them saw that truck all tore up."

"I said no talking about it. Now go to bed."

"Dad-deee," he whined.

"Go on, now." Al scooped up the flat cherry and scraped it off the fork with his teeth.

After Caleb left the room, Margaret smiled at Al. "How you like the cake, hon?"

"Good."

Since Margaret was trying to steer the conversation away from the blast, Lum announced that she was going to bed.

Once in her little room, she untied the tablecloth, took out Dan's suits, and spread them on the quilt, running her hands over them and feeling in the pockets, the slick fabric sometimes snagging against her rough fingers. Matchboxes with a few matches rattling around, coins, and calling cards. She imagined Dan shaking hands, taking the other man's card and tucking it away without any intention of looking at it again. She unbuttoned her dress and stepped out of it. After hanging it on a nail in the wall, she pulled a suit coat on her bare arm, the cold muslin raising her arm hair. She slipped into the other sleeve and pulled the coat across her chest. Rubbing her hand against the nubby wool, she heard the unmistakable sound of ripping fabric. Darn! Intending to only feel the sleeve against her skin, she couldn't stop, but had to pull it on completely.

Only a small rip showed on a side seam. After a quick whipstitch it would be suitable for the church sale. She folded the jacket and bundled up all the suits. She wouldn't touch them again. Just hand them over to the church ladies and look for something that would fit. Something as nice as what she was swapping. She wondered if she would be able to talk like a man if anyone at the roadhouse spoke to her. She would have to remember to stay away from topics like baby remedies and cooking.

A Fitting Suit

1933

When Lum saw the soft snow floating down, she prayed she'd find new shoes. The soles of the ones she was wearing were so thin that if the snow stuck to the ground, the ball of her left foot would be soaked. If only she hadn't bought so many postcards, she might have enough money for shoes. But she hadn't known she'd be walking down High Ford Road to town every day. Once they turned it into the scenic parkway, would she be able to walk down the middle of the road like she did now? Or would cars be going in two directions all the time? She rarely saw a car heading up the mountain, but farmers' trucks went by every now and then.

She had made breakfast extra early and put it in the warming tray since Caleb wasn't up yet. Al seemed in a good enough mood that she was happy to leave him and Margaret alone so she could be one of the first people at the swap meet. Margaret would have to come up with a story as to why Lum wasn't there for supper.

She dreaded tramping through snow to the roadhouse and back. What had she agreed to? For the sake of Margaret and Al's marriage, she'd reassure Margaret that Al didn't have a girlfriend. At least, she assumed that she'd find him with men and no evidence of a dalliance with a woman. Then maybe they wouldn't have their daily fight about Al going out after supper. It was the least and most she could do. She couldn't fix Al's temper or Margaret's changing moods.

As she hurried across the square with the bag of clothes slung over her shoulder, she noticed that Lord Fairfax had a coating of white hair today, and the little pond had a light layer of ice topped with snow.

At the church, the aroma of freshly brewed coffee greeted her.

"Good morning," chirped a short woman in a slick brown coat.

"Morning," Lum replied. "I have some clothes to swap."

"We done set up the clothes yesterday."

"But some ladies told me I could bring them today." Lum's eyes swept the church for someone she knew but didn't see anyone familiar.

"No, we finished setting up last night." The church lady turned away.

"Wait. It's men's suits. Nice ones. From a banker."

The woman turned back. "In that case, I reckon we can take 'em." She held out her arms. "See Miss Benson for a receipt." She pointed with her chin toward a table.

"Thank you." The coffee sure smelled good, even though she'd hurriedly drunk a cup before leaving Al and Margaret's. Her bladder felt full. People stood around tables, holding up dresses and pants, checking lengths and seams, testing zippers. She didn't hear anyone mention the explosion. Maybe they all thought it was part of the roadwork. She might have thought so herself except for Braxton and Al's reactions. For Al to tell her not to say anything around town almost sounded like he had something to hide.

After getting credit for four suits, Lum looked for men's clothes. The men's table was piled with overalls, but most were worn thin about the knees and backside. If she showed up at the roadhouse as a farmer, folks would expect to know who he was. Could she dress like a road worker? They were all so young and they all wore those brown uniforms like Kenny's. As she was digging through piles, the short woman came over with Dan's folded and priced suits.

"You looking for more clothes for your banker?"

Lum shook her head. "Clothes like that but a bigger size."

"We put the church-type clothes over here." This time she pointed with an elbow. Lum headed to the stack of suits. This would be just right. A respectable man in a suit, like those Yankees at the meeting. Her fingers did the searching, feeling linen, wool, heavy cotton. A heavy twill fabric appealed to her, but the pants were too short. *Size*, she thought, *size first, then texture.* She found a nice brown herringbone suit with minute flecks of blue that looked like it would fit. Thick, nubby wool for a wintry day. The wool felt soft yet a little scratchy, like her chin by nightfall. She looked around, furtively held the pants to her waist, making sure they were wide enough. The coat was double-breasted. Would it hide her bosom? She couldn't wait to put it on. Her bladder urged her to empty it, so she headed for the church bathroom.

Inside, she locked the door, yanked her dress up to her waist, and kicked off the soggy shoes. Still seated after urinating, she pulled the pants on, and standing, she slipped her hand into the pocket, which had a tiny hole in the corner. She stuck her finger through it and felt her leg. The intense throbbing she felt when she rubbed herself arose, but she wasn't touching her tender parts. Only the crotch of the pants brushed against her underpants. The wide legs, tight through the thighs and loose against her calves, caressed her. Is this what men felt every day? No wonder they chased women. She slipped on the jacket, pleased that the buttons could close without her hearing that ripping sound. Quickly she took off the suit, squeezed her feet into wet shoes, folded the suit and went back out. One of the church ladies said, "You're not supposed to take the clothes into the bathroom."

Lum blushed. "I didn't know." Her heart was still beating rapidly.

The woman held out her arms. "You want me to hold that for you while you look around?"

"No!" she snapped, hugging the suit. In a softer tone she asked, "Any shoes?"

"That way."

After rummaging, Lum found two pairs of shoes that fit—black ones for men, and a brown pair of women's—some men's socks, and a white shirt to wear with the herringbone suit. She also got three dresses for Meg, a shirt for Caleb, two sunbonnets, one of which she'd give to Margaret, a hat for Al, and handkerchiefs she'd give to Jimmy and Walter. She thought about getting something for Dan, but worried that he wouldn't want anything used. Just as she was leaving, she saw a pile of books. She dug through it and was excited to find one by Jack London, *The Call of the Wild*. She'd get it for Dan, since he liked *White Fang* so much. For herself she got copies of *The Adventures of Huckleberry Finn*, *Little Men*, and *Jo's Boys*. So much to read!

At the exit, a church lady said, "Credit's only good for clothes. Books are one cent a piece."

Lum fished a nickel out of her blouse and paid. She'd never thought of books as something to buy, but rather as things that were already in folks' houses. She exited the church carrying two bulky bags. As she descended the granite steps, Nancy and Myra Collins from Hopkin's Knob passed her, wearing thin coats.

"No coloreds until after noon," one of the church ladies said sternly.

"We're not colored," Myra replied.

"You know the rules," the church member claimed.

"We're as white as you are."

"Come back after noon," another lady said, smiling. "We'll have plenty of clothes left."

Nancy put her hand on her hip. "We just walked down here in the snow. What we gonna do for three hours in this town? It's too cold to sit in the park, and that ol' biddy at the store won't sell us nothing."

"We can't make exceptions, or everyone will want to come in the morning."

"We ain't coming back!" Nancy spat the words.

Ordinarily, Lum would have been sympathetic to the Melungeons being treated this way, but these two were the wives of the Collins men who had threatened Kenny. Suddenly she felt ashamed. It wasn't their fault what their husbands did. That would be like blaming Margaret for Al's actions. She was reminded of the explosion and how he and Walter had looked at each other. She turned around and called up the steps.

"For goodness sakes," Lum said, "these women walked all the way down here through the snow, you can at least let them in."

"I'll thank you to mind your own business," the church lady replied.

"I'm a member of this church, so it is my business."

The church lady said, "All right, why don't you two come in out of the cold. You can start shopping in about an hour."

"Thankee," the older Collins said.

Lum smiled to herself. Sometimes people did listen to her. For the first time that day, she wondered about Kenny. Where did he sleep last night? He had sounded so sure he couldn't go back to the Knob. Last she'd seen him he'd been going to look for Mr. Shapiro. What had happened to him?

When she arrived at the Shays' house, Liza opened the door with a welcoming smile. Lum had forgotten that Liza wouldn't be teaching since it was Saturday. "Daddy's sleeping. Since you're here, I think I'll go to the library. Can you watch the chicken broth?"

When it was done, Lum strained the broth and picked the tender chicken meat from the bones, chopped it, and rolled out long sheets of dough she had prepared. While cutting long sheets of egg noodles, she worried about wearing the suit, trying to blend in with the crowd at the roadhouse and not be recognized. What would the men do if they discovered a woman dressed like a man? Could she really get away with this?

She puzzled over the explosion last night. Who did it, and why? Obviously someone wanted to stop the road. Al and Walter? But they'd been right in front of her when it happened. A worker who'd been fired? A Melungeon? From Kenny's telling, his people sounded mad about the road. Why didn't Kenny come back to see Al? Did he go home after he spent the night in her room and get shot? Or was he hiding from the Collinses? She remembered him in his fresh uniform; him standing up at the town meeting; peering in her room; talking fondly about his early life on the Knob; and the feeling she'd had with his feet tucked under her.

She concentrated on cutting straight lines in the noodle dough with the paring knife, but now her thoughts turned to imagining what it would be like to walk into the roadhouse. The more she thought about it the scarier it seemed. She should have stuck with her first instinct—to refuse. And now, where could she change into the suit? When she decided to do it here, she hadn't thought about walking out past Dan and Liza wearing a man's suit. She usually thought things through, but she'd never done anything like this. Dress up like a man to enter a strange place—never. She couldn't back out, though, she'd given Margaret her word. She had decided a long time ago to just do what was asked and not worry about the future, because the future was always in someone else's hands and worrying did no good. She'd go to the roadhouse, find out if Al had a girlfriend, and leave. And hope no one recognized her.

"You came to see me on Saturday?"

Startled, Lum jumped at Dan's voice. Turning around, she noticed him wearing royal blue pajama bottoms and a long-sleeved white undershirt.

"I forgot Liza would be here," she mumbled.

"I don't mind two women looking out for me, I reckon."

"When I got here, she left for the library, so I'm finishing up the soup. Thought I'd make some noodles." Lum wiped her floury hands on her apron, rustled in a bag, and pulled out the green cloth book embossed with three pictures of a dog sled team on the cover. Shyly, she handed it to him, saying, "This is for you."

"*Call of the Wild*? For me? You didn't have to do this."

"I wanted to. After all, if you hadn't given me those suits I couldn't'a gotten all these clothes." As soon as she said it, she regretted mentioning the clothes. But he didn't ask what else she got, so she showed him the books she got herself.

"You finished *Moby Dick*?"

"No, I left it here." She hoped he'd offer to let her take it home.

"Now you got you a stack of books. Doesn't that make you feel rich?"

She nodded. She'd started reading *The Adventures of Huckleberry Finn* as a child, but Jimmy had hidden it from her after saying it was a boy's book. The poor book was probably in the barn now, ruined rather than read by a girl. If only there were a barn nearby where she could change her clothes. She dreaded this whole ordeal even though she wanted to feel that suit again. Realizing Dan was talking about the blast from the night before, she scrambled to figure out what he had just said since he seemed to be waiting for an answer.

"You sure are preoccupied today," he remarked.

"Oh." She returned to cutting noodles, but her hand was shaking.

"Stop messing with that dough a minute." He pulled out a chair. "Sit."

Wiping her hands on her apron, she sat at the table like a chastened child.

"You're worried about something, aren't you?" His hazel eyes looked green.

She nodded, not used to such kindness. A lump was forming in her throat. She didn't know where to begin. "There's a lot to worry about."

"Like what?"

Words tumbled out—Al losing the farm, Kenny's situation, Margaret's suspicions, until he held up a hand.

"You're talking about other people. What's worrying *you*— Columbia Carson?"

Tears. Silly tears caused from hearing her own name. Did he really want to hear about *her*? She tried to blot her wet eyes with the back of her hand, not wanting to be obvious. Concentrating on a deep line that ran between his eyebrows, she began again, this time about what would happen to her if Al and her brothers lost their farms, and about not wanting to work in a mill.

"But what's bothering you so much today?"

She looked down at her flour-dusted apron. "Something Margaret asked me to do. Tonight."

He just nodded encouragingly.

"You may hate me when I tell you this. You may never want me in your house again. But it was Margaret's idea. And I agreed to it. . ." She swallowed.

Lum stared at herself in the mirror, amazed at how the heavy wool jacket with wide lapels obscured her breasts, making her look barrel-chested. She viewed her profile. At this angle, too, she appeared to be a heavyset man. She toyed with the black bowler hat Dan had suggested she wear. He said it was the height of fashion to wear black shoes and a black hat with a brown suit. She strode across Liza's bedroom, feeling the swish of wool against her legs.

When she came out, Dan was also wearing a suit. "I'm not letting you go down there by yourself. Let me drive you."

"It's not up to you to let me do anything, Dan." Wearing the suit made her feel powerful.

"Probably no one will bother you. But if they do, wouldn't you rather not be alone?"

He'd be next to useless in a fight, but she had to admit he was right about her going to the roadhouse alone. "Oh, all right, but don't blame me if you have a cough tomorrow. It's cold as Christmas out there."

"I haven't been out of the house in weeks. I'm about to go stir-crazy." He paused. "You look mighty fine in that suit, but you need a tie." He disappeared into his bedroom and came out with a black-and-blue-striped tie. Standing close, he tied it around her neck and tucked a white handkerchief into her breast pocket.

In the car, Lum rested her hands on her woolen thighs. Dan pulled the choke and the car sputtered for a while, but to her relief and disappointment it roared to life.

"You sure Al will be there tonight?" he asked.

"I'd be mighty surprised if he's not, especially after that explosion. I'm sure all the men will be talking about it." She felt the back of her neck to make sure her hair bun was hidden by the hat. "I hope nobody recognizes me."

"I'll say you're my business partner. Tell the truth, I want to go there to tell the road workers about my boarding house."

"When are your houses gonna be ready?"

"Soon as I can get them fixed up some. I might divide some of the rooms to get more folks in, but I can't wait too long. Men are pouring into town to work."

Could she ask about the cooks? Maybe he had already hired some pretty young women that the men would like. Why was she even thinking about it? She couldn't let her family down. Jimmy and Ethel were counting on her returning next month.

"Dan?" she said timidly.

"Uh-huh?"

"I'm glad you're coming with me. I don't know how I thought I'd go in by myself."

"Don't mention it." He paused and scratched his ear. "When I was young, another fellow and I would go to New York to see the shows on weekends. He knew about secret clubs where men dressed like women and sometimes there would be women wearing men's clothing. I wasn't always sure who was who in those situations."

"Really?" She stared at his profile. "There are places like that?"

He nodded. "It was fun helping you get ready tonight." He slowed down and turned off the road by a long white building with lots of trucks and cars parked in front.

"So this is where Al comes every night." She stepped out, feet comfortable in the roomy men's shoes. "Think we'll see any floozies?"

"A couple of good-looking guys like us . . ." He winked.

Was he really starting to think of her as a man? She drew in a deep breath as they reached the door. "This is it."

Loud voices and smoky air greeted them. They stood for a minute, and Lum tried to focus through the smoky darkness. Men sat at long tables, eating out of steaming bowls next to mugs containing various amounts of amber-hued liquid. Once her eyes adjusted, she looked for Al, but didn't see him or her brothers. Relieved that they weren't there, she followed Dan to a table. He approached two men in the brown uniforms of the Road Commission who looked barely twenty years old; their faces were tanned but still soft-cheeked, and their hands, holding big soup spoons, were rough, but still had the plumpness of youth. One had a thin gold band on his left ring finger.

"Can we sit here?" Dan asked.

The man with a ring said, "Sure. You want some chili, go up front, they got big ol' pots of it."

Lum's eyes burned from all the smoke, but she and Dan found the chili.

"Help yourselves," a tall woman said. "It's made with venison. Best meat for chili."

"How much?" Lum didn't have to be embarrassed about her deep voice as she ladled the thick chili into a bowl. *Some cornbread would be good with this*, she thought.

"On the house, sir. Go on up to the bar if you want a drink."

Lum realized she could take as wide a stride as she wanted without being caught by the hem of a skirt. They returned to the table and sat down by the young road workers. Dan brought two beers and when he set one in front of her, she shook her head and pushed it towards him.

"Where y'all from?" Dan asked.

"North Carolina. Me and my brother, here, we worked on the road near home and followed the crew. Better than joining the CCC."

"Where you staying?"

"With this nice couple that's children's grown. We got one of their bedrooms and we can use their kitchen, but we don't know nothing about cooking, so we come here." He looked at them again. "Y'all don't cook neither? Not married?"

"I'm a widower. Dan Shay. This here's my business partner, Mr. Columbus."

Lum nodded, thinking the chili sure could use some seasoning.

"Pleased to meet you. I'm Ronnie Eldridge, and this here's my brother, Nick."

Dan said, "I wanted to meet some of you fellows and see if anyone needed a place to stay. I'm opening a boarding house, meals included, so you won't have to live off of chili."

Ronnie laughed. "Sure am getting tired of it."

Dan continued, "I know a lady who's an excellent cook. I'm hoping I can persuade her to take a job, but I don't know if her family will let her go."

Lum jerked her head from the chili bowl. Did he mean her? Or was he just making conversation? Or teasing her, knowing her family wouldn't allow it? But hadn't she decided to start making her own decisions?

"What do you think, Mr. Columbus?" Dan coughed.

She whispered, "All this smoke isn't good for you, Dan. You been doing so much better, but this may set you back."

"Nonsense." He coughed again, this time into his handkerchief.

The door burst open, and Walter, Jimmy, Al, and a few other men rushed in. Shouts erupted from a round table full of men in overalls as they joined them. Lum's heart started pounding. What if they saw her? What could she say? She'd never hear the end of it. Al might even make her leave, and Walter and Jimmy—no telling what they'd do. Once Ethel found out, she'd tell the whole town. *Make them stay away*, she prayed. Nick and Ronnie groaned.

"Who are those guys?" Lum pulled the brim of the hat down, but then worried about her bun showing in back, so she touched her neck, hoping the wisps of hair weren't visible in the dark. Al and Walter were sitting at the round table now, so she could breathe easier.

"Troublemakers." Nick's lip curled on the left side. "Always trying to pick fights with us workers. Telling us to go back where we came from, stuff like that. Some of the guys have gotten into fistfights with 'em."

Lum prayed they wouldn't come over to harass Nick and Ronnie. If they did, surely they'd recognize her.

Ronnie leaned closer. "Some say they're behind that blast last night."

"That big explosion?" Lum lowered her head in case Al or her brother looked her way.

"Yep. They're always whispering amongst theirselves if they're not taunting us, so we figured they were planning something, because they'd say stuff like if we didn't leave we'd be sorry. We always go in pairs 'cause we think they might try to jump us or something."

Nick said, "One thing we can't figure out: there's supposed to be a night watchman around that equipment, ol' Sam Hayes. Nobody's seen him. Some folks say whoever done it kidnapped him, some say he was blown to smithereens, others say he was bribed to not be there that night and he took off with the money."

Dan started coughing, a rasping cough that sounded like he couldn't catch his breath.

Lum was glad for an excuse to leave. "We better get going," she said. "My friend shouldn't be in such a smoky place."

"One more question," Dan recovered enough to say. "Any fast women come here?" He swallowed some beer.

"Ha!" Nick laughed. "Miss Berry, the owner there," he indicated the woman by the chili. "She don't 'low none of that. You want to find some women, go behind the mill late at night."

Lum was glad Dan hadn't forgotten her purpose for being there.

"You ever see any of those troublemaker guys with women?" he asked.

"I wouldn't know, but they're always here, so I don't know when they'd have a chance."

"Come on, Dan," Lum urged. She didn't want to risk Al or one of her brothers coming over to harass the workers and seeing her or

Dan. They seemed to be having a good time, like they were celebrating something, but she knew it was only a matter of time until they turned mean. While Dan told the brothers how to find his boarding house, Lum waited by the door.

"You want me to carry you home, or would you like to come to my house?" he asked.

"I left my clothes and things at your house, but then I'll need to go home. Margaret will be waiting up for my report."

"All right." He paused. "How about a little coffee?"

He must be lonely, and after all he'd done to make this venture easier, it was the least she could do to keep him company a little longer. Margaret wouldn't expect her this early. "Coffee would be nice. But I don't want Liza to see me."

"I doubt she's home yet. She and that librarian like to play cards and listen to the radio programs on Saturdays. It's her one night she stays out late."

When they got back to Dan's, Lum added water to the coffee pot, lit the stove and placed two china cups on the table. Dan was talking about his plans for the boarding houses. When the coffee was ready, Lum sat across from him, crossing her leg with her ankle resting on the knee. She could easily get used to men's clothes. If he would only mention the cook he needed again, she'd speak up. Could she really leave her family? Would she even be able to ask him if he'd hire her? He seemed to be thinking out loud, adding up how much he could charge for a room, the total number of rooms, and what he'd have to do to get ready.

"Dan," she interrupted. If she didn't ask now she may never have the courage again. The worst he could say was "no." Heart pounding, she forged ahead. "Have you hired cooks?"

A smile played at the corners of his mouth. "I haven't advertised for one yet." He sipped, and set his cup in the saucer. "I'll have to see how many applicants I get."

She hadn't thought about him interviewing people. "I thought you said you had someone in mind."

"Oh, I do. I just don't know if she'd be interested in living in a house full of men and cooking for lots of folks." His green-flecked eyes flashed in the lamplight.

Was it her or someone else? "Who you thinking about? Someone from Staunton?"

"No, not Staunton. Here." He leaned toward her. "Miss Columbia, would you like to cook at my boarding house?"

"I think so." Her hand started shaking. "Let's talk about it."

"I'll pay you a salary, and you can have your pick of the rooms at the boarding house."

She couldn't say anything for fear she would cry. She could be a working woman, with wages. Now she had to get the courage to tell her family.

Fishing

1907

With thick thumb and forefinger, Lum's father pulled an earthworm from the bucket. Lum and Jimmy had dug them from under a rock. There was something satisfying about lifting a rock and seeing the worms, small and large, wriggling close to the surface. Easy to get enough to go fishing. Even in the bucket, they smelled of dark, leafy soil.

Her daddy speared the worm with the fishing hook. When he handed it to Lum he said, "Go on and catch another one. So far, you've caught the most today."

"I'll get one 'fore you," Walter said as he cast his pole again.

Lum flicked her wrist to land the bait in the water. She knew that Walter let his sink too low. She had better luck when she let the worm float right below the surface.

"I'm gonna catch a big 'un," Guthrie said. "Not little bitty ones like Lummy's catching."

Lum liked the sweet, tender bluegills. Granny would dredge them through cornmeal and fry them in the large cast iron skillet along with the corn fritters. The older boys liked the larger bass, but Lum couldn't figure why they always thought bigger fish were better when they didn't taste as good.

She stood with feet apart, feeling solidly grounded in the mucky riverbank. She felt a slight tug on her line, so she pulled, but it dipped down, bending the pole. She tightened her grip, determined to not let the fish get loose.

"Ho!" her father called out. "You got you a big one this time."

Guthrie came toward her. "Want me to haul it in?"

"No." *I'll do it myself,* she thought. *I'll show them I'm just as good, if not a better, fisherman.*

"She can't do it!" Jimmy yelled.

"Let her try," Daddy said. He sidestepped toward her. She felt his warmth, his own smell, now like fish, but also like rich dirt, the kind that produced earthworms.

"Just pull steady against his strength. Slowly, but show him you're in charge."

She lifted her arms over her head, both hands tight on the pole.

"Put your arms straight ahead from your chest," Daddy urged. "You don't need to lift until it comes close."

The line was still being tugged and Lum jerked it back, all of a sudden feeling lightness where there had been resistance. The line was limp, but she didn't want to accept the idea that the fish got away.

"Oh, dang!" Guthrie said. "Told you I should'a done it for ya."

"Son," her daddy said. "You don't know you could'a done it no better. She did just fine."

"Yeah, but . . ."

"But nothing. Here, Lum, let's get you another worm. We know there's a foxy fish in there. That's how he got so big, not getting caught."

"I'm gonna catch him," Walter bragged.

"Not if I do first," Jimmy said.

"I'm gonna get him again 'cause I already got him once," Lum said.

Daddy clapped her on the shoulder. "You might, or one of the boys will. Or even me. But sometimes the fish gets away."

Family Objections
1933

In Dan's car, Lum carried her dress balled up in the sack with the other clothes from the rummage sale. After Dan let her out, Lum hurried into her room so no one would see her in the suit. But she didn't want to take it off, not yet, not until she and the suit were alone together. She stroked the wool crotch. When she couldn't stand it any more, she pushed the pants to her knees, rubbing her part that was too long for a woman but too short for a man, thinking about the night Kenny slept in her room, and how she'd felt with his feet under her.

She didn't sleep well and got up when she heard the roosters and saw the sun peeking through the dusty window. She had to tell Margaret the good news about Al, if it was good news. At least he wasn't with a woman—but how much could she tell? That he was suspected of setting off dynamite? Was it true, or were the workers out for revenge for his taunting? Still, Al had acted so strange the night of the explosion. And Walter. There was definitely something fishy going on.

She felt the fabric of the folded suit one last time before putting it into the valise. Maybe there would be another opportunity to wear it. But when? She snapped the valise shut and headed to the kitchen.

She quickly told Margaret: No women in the roadhouse except for the stern owner, certainly no floozies allowed. She had seen Al—yes, he was drinking and having a good time. She couldn't help but tell her about Al threatening the workers, but Margaret pooh-poohed it.

"Oh, that's just Al," Margaret said. After a minute, she asked, "They said he's there every night?"

"They said they didn't know when him or Walter had time for a woman because they were always at the roadhouse."

"I reckon I feel relieved then. It's just . . . Caleb's mama wasn't dead yet when he started courting me, so I didn't know."

"He's devoted to you, but he has a lot on his mind now."

Margaret looked away. "Things got better that night, you know, after the explosion."

Lum had thought Margaret and Al seemed closer the morning after the blast. "I got y'all some things from the rumble, um, rummage sale." She brought in the bag of clothes and was surprised to find *Moby Dick*. When had Dan slipped it in? After Margaret exclaimed over the new items, she urged Caleb and Al to hurry up for church.

Caleb and Lum rode in the back of the truck. Caleb was eager to go to Sunday school to talk about the explosion until Lum reminded him that Al forbade him to mention it.

The minister greeted all newcomers, especially government officials and road workers. She dreaded telling her family about her job. Would they be relieved that she'd no longer be a burden, or would they miss all the ways she helped out? When Braxton stood and asked for prayers for his daddy, she realized she'd been preoccupied through all the songs, Bible readings, and prayers.

She listened to the sermon. The minister stood, fingers interlaced, hands over his ample middle. "It is God's will to build a road through His creation so that man can enjoy and have dominion over nature. For are we not stewards of the land? God's bounty must be shared with our poor, unfortunate brethren who moved away to toil in cities and towns. God is leading them like lost sheep to our lovely mountains. How can we claim the beauty only for ourselves? God's abundance must be shared and loved by all His creatures."

The minister lowered his voice. "The Devil reveres death, destruction, and evil. The Devil is responsible for the evil in men's hearts. The men who set off dynamite must let Jesus Christ enter their hearts and souls. It was a terrible, evil act, but small evils are performed every day. Sins that don't light up the sky, but blacken our souls and separate us from God. All of us are sinners, but we can be forgiven by God, the merciful, through his only begotten Son who suffered upon the cross for our sins."

Some farmers sitting in front of Lum were squirming in their seats. She noticed some of the congregation looking around. Lum was sitting next to Al, but she didn't dare look at him. Jimmy and Ethel were next to Margaret, on the other side of Al. Walter didn't come to church often. She resolved to tell them all about her job right after church. She tried to prepare what she would say, then came back to the present. The minister went on to describe the agonies of hell, but Lum worried more about what would happen to whoever set off the dynamite if the sheriff, rather than the Lord, found out who it was.

While the minister called for folks to be saved, the organist played "Softly and Tenderly Jesus is Calling," and Lum hoped someone would go forward before what seemed like thirty-two verses were played. Finally, an elderly couple of die-hard Baptists went forward to rededicate their lives. Lum doubted they were the dynamite culprits. Had the preacher really expected whoever was guilty to come forward?

Afterward, people stood around talking about the blasts while the Welcoming Committee members tried to nab the workers, urging them to come back Wednesday for Prayer Meeting. Lum stuck close to Margaret and didn't let Jimmy and Ethel out of her sight. She wanted to talk to her family before she lost her nerve since Dan said the house would be ready in a few days.

When they'd stopped talking to some neighbors, Lum said, "Jimmy, Margaret, all of you, I need to tell you something."

Al was clustered with some of the other farmers, but Margaret pulled him away. "Al, Lum wants to say something."

"Can't she tell us at dinner?"

Lum shook her head. "I need to tell Jimmy and Ethel, too."

"Shoot," Jimmy said, pointing his index finger at her throat.

"Ethel and Jimmy, you know it's almost time for me to come stay with y'all." She was trembling. She imagined wool pants warming her cold legs. "I won't be able to. I've got a job."

Al laughed. "A job?"

"Who'd hire *you*?" Ethel asked.

"Dan Shay."

Margaret scratched her head. "He's gonna need you all the time? What's the matter with him?"

"He's getting better. I'm not gonna be taking care of him, it's a real job."

"Oh, he's just fooling with you, don't you know that?" Jimmy sneered.

Lum felt her face warming. "No, he's not!"

"What'll you be doin'?" Margaret asked.

"What I do best. I'm gonna cook at Dan's boarding house for road workers."

"Saw him at the roadhouse last night." Al rubbed the back of his neck. "At first I thought it was some Feds. I wondered what him and another stiff in a business suit were doing there. Now I know, they were trying to get boarders."

So he had seen her. And called her a stiff. She thought she and Dan made a dapper pair, but they'd stood out compared to the other men in overalls and highway uniforms. She was glad they'd left when they did.

"You can't do that." Jimmy blew into his hands.

"Why not?" Her eyes felt scratchy from the smoky bar and lack of sleep.

"Your family needs you," Jimmy replied.

"You-all can get by without me. You do when I'm not there, don't you?"

"You can't be around all them strange men," Al objected.

"I'm bigger'n most of 'em. They won't mess with me." She took a wider stance, the suit stance. She should have known her family wouldn't believe she could do anything on her own.

"Where will you live?" Margaret asked.

"A room comes with the job."

"Lummy, we'll miss you, 'specially me," Margaret said. "I won't have nobody to talk to."

"I'll be right here on Adams Street. I'll still see you at church and can come visit."

"It won't be the same." Margaret stuck out her bottom lip. "What about Meg?"

Lum worried. Would Meg get her medicine?

"She'll be back," Al reassured his wife. "Road workers won't be here forever."

"Then the boarding house will become an inn for tourists," Lum explained.

"Big plans," Jimmy scoffed.

Ethel put her hand on Lum's arm. "Don't worry, we'll take you in if it don't work out."

She could never hold her head up if she had to come back to them after starting to work.

"Lum, working's not the same as being with family," Al said. "You'll see."

No, you'll *see*, she thought. *The old Lum would've given in and said, yes, it was a wild idea. Other people had jobs, not me. But the old Lum wouldn't have even considered having a job.* She remembered the woman who owned the roadhouse and told fancy ladies they couldn't ply their trade there. *If that woman can own a bar, I can certainly do what I've done all my life—cook for people.*

Condemned

1933

On Monday Lum wasn't sure if she should go to Dan's or stay with Margaret. She had stayed up late reading *Moby Dick* and wanted to talk to him about it. He had kidded her that all the books she got at the rummage sale were children's books, but she hadn't had a chance to read them as a child, so she wanted to find out what happened to Huck and Jim and what Jo was like as a mother of boys.

Since she hadn't told Dan she wouldn't be at his house, she supposed she should at least drop in. Maybe if he felt well enough, they could go see the boarding house on Adams. But when Lum said she was going to check on Dan, Margaret pouted, "Reckon I better get used to not having no help."

Lum felt like she'd been slapped. Yesterday she'd thought Margaret was really going to miss *her*, not just her help.

Although the wind felt cold, there was no sign of snow, just a thin layer of frost melting in the sun. She was only a little way along when she saw a small square sign: "Condemned, Order of the U.S. Road Commission." On Al's land! They posted the sign away from the pasture, so Al wouldn't see it for a day or so unless he headed into town, and he wouldn't see it at night. She had to tell him right away. Plodding back up the road, she was nearly exhausted from the uphill climb when she saw him throwing hay to the cows. Waving frantically, she finally caught his attention.

"What is it?" he panted, out of breath from running to the fence. "Margie? The baby?"

"Al, there's a sign. Your land is condemned by the Road Commission."

"Yankee bastards! I knew they were out to get me!" Al pounded a fence post. "Think they can steal my land? I'll sue 'em. This'll be tied up in the courts 'til their beards are white."

"Good for you!" Just as she'd found a new place, now the family was losing their home. She turned toward the road, hoping they wouldn't feel like she abandoned them.

"Where you off to?" He glared at her.

"Gonna check in on Dan." She had to know for sure that he wasn't just teasing about the job, like Jimmy said.

"Wait 'til I put on a clean shirt, and I'll carry you to town. I'm going down to that Resettlement Office. They're not gonna resettle *my* family."

"I'd appreciate it." She hadn't looked forward to walking down the icy road.

When they were riding along, Lum asked, "Seen Kenny lately?"

Al jerked his head at the name. "Kenny?" He looked straight ahead. "Why?"

"Ain't seen him around lately, that's all."

"Didn't know you cared about him." Al sped up.

"Oh, I don't. Not really. Just anxious 'cause he came by Thursday night worried the Collinses would kill him. They called him a traitor for trying to get them to sell their homes. He said he needed to talk to you." Lum wished Al would slow down. Even if he knew every curve on the road, he could misjudge and they'd fall over a cliff. She added, "I was worried those Collinses got him or something."

"He's probably just hiding somewhere." Al continued, "You know who *is* a damned traitor? That preacher. I almost walked out yesterday when he was saying the highway is God's will. What a bunch of bullshit! Oh, sorry, Lum. He's on the take, mark my words." The truck's tires squealed as he rounded another curve. "He can take his Hell and go to it."

She'd better find a safe topic, or else they'd go flying off one of the steep curves. "I got a copy of *The Adventures of Huckleberry Finn*. You think Caleb would like to read it?"

"He don't much like reading."

They were on the highway, passing tobacco fields that had been picked clean until spring plantings. She wondered what Snell would do about all those sharecroppers living in cabins that would be destroyed for the scenic highway.

"Where's this Dan Shay fella live?" Al asked when they entered town.

"Oh, I'll get out at the square. I want to walk down Adams, see if I can figure out which house I'll be working at."

Al didn't reply, just pulled up in front of the Resettlement Office, which still had "hen Harper" on the glass front. Deputy Gleason walked up to the truck and leaned down to the window, prominent ears pointing heavenward.

"Howdy, folks."

"Morning, Deputy." Al looked up.

"We caught the one blew up the road equipment."

"Which one?" Al's voice shook.

"Friend of yours." Gleason rested his palms on the window opening. "That ex-con."

"Kenny?" Lum gasped.

"Yep. We thought for sure it was planned by other men, but he kept saying, 'I lit it.'"

"But he was working for the Scenic," Lum insisted. "Don't make sense, does it, Al?" Then she recalled Kenny saying he was on Al's side.

Red crept up Al's neck and onto his cheeks.

The deputy's head came further into the truck. "With his record, he'll be going back to prison for sure. Them Melungeons sure are tight-lipped. They'd rather kill a man than turn him in. Can you imagine, Al?"

Al shook his head. Lum noticed sweat beading up on his upper lip although the open window let in a cool draft around the deputy's body.

Gleason continued, "That night watchman don't show up, your friend might just get charged with murder. Shame, ain't it?"

All the color drained from Al's face.

"Just imagine what will happen to a man charged with two murders. Why, they might even—"

Lum leaned over Al toward the deputy, interrupting. "Can we visit him in jail?" She had to see him. If he'd been put up to it, maybe she could convince him to tell the truth.

"Not here no more. What he confessed to is a federal offense, destroying government property. Sheriff's driving him to Richmond to wait for his trial. Won't be no bail." He pulled his head out of the window. Hitting the top of Al's truck, he said, "Y'all take care, now."

When the deputy was out of sight, Al rested his forehead on the steering wheel. "Them Collinses shouldn't'a called him a traitor. He's the most loyal man I know."

Kenny had said he was indebted to Al. Those mountain men always paid their debts. She had to get away from Al right now, or she might tell him who *she thought* was a traitor. Lum opened the car door and without looking at him said, "Good-bye, Al." When she was halfway across the street she heard the car door slam. She turned around and saw him, shoulders slumped, heading toward the Resettlement Office.

She imagined Kenny in the backseat of the sheriff's car, silently watching the fields shorn of tobacco. Was he thinking about reuniting with his daddy and brother? She'd probably never see Kenny again, that black lock she had wanted to brush out of his eyes. All she had were their brief conversations and the feeling she'd had with his feet under her the night before he lit the fuse. Had he known that night that he was going to do it? Was it an attempt to redeem himself with the Portugee he felt he'd betrayed? Was he really taking the fall for other men? The men she'd grown up with? She didn't know how she could ever look at Al again. Or her brothers. Suddenly she remembered them mocking Clyde Jackson hanging from the tree, their tongues out and heads askew, holding up three fingers.

She turned down Adams Street, looking for an empty house. In front of a three-story Victorian with a rounded porch and a large turret on the left corner, she saw Dan, idly picking paint flakes off the porch railing. He had a long muffler wrapped around his neck and tucked inside a heavy coat. A hat covered his ears.

"Good morning, Miss Columbia." The hand that had been flaking paint went to his neck. "Before you fuss at me for being outside, my throat and chest are wrapped warmly, see?"

"Yes, I see. Good to know you listen to me, at least a little."

"I'm meeting the painters. Soon as we get it painted, you can move in."

So the painters were coming today. She'd have her own room in a fine house, freshly painted, not a drafty, neglected porch room. But that was where Kenny had spent the night, possibly the last safe place he'd been. She wished she could have kept him there, out of trouble.

She'd have to stay at Al's a night or two longer, knowing that his children might lose the only home they'd ever known. Then she'd pack up the suit, her dresses, books, and postcards: Daisy, Violet, the Fat Lady, the Tattooed Man, the Hindoo, and all the others, some missing body parts, some with extra appendages. In her new home, she could unpack for good.

He opened the front door. She looked around the empty house. "Dan," she said, "I know where you can get some nice antiques for a good price. Smiley can get you anything you want."

"I'd like to see what he has. You want to come pick out your room?"

"Sure do—but first, I want to see the kitchen."

Side Show

1934

To think she would be getting postcards for Smiley, Lum mused as she walked to Dan's home. Last week when she'd gone to the fair with Al and Margaret and Caleb, she'd been denied entrance to the tent with Manfred/Matilda, the Half-Man/Half-Woman. Tonight she'd see what was in the "men only" tent.

Daffodils and tulips lined the walkway to Dan's house. Lum carried the valise that held the man's suit. The newspaper clippings and postcards had their own place in her room in the boarding house where she'd lived for six months. She and Dan had gone together in their suits to Roanoke and Staunton a few times. Dan liked to visit lodges, and she was always curious about what type of food was being prepared. At first she wore a dress, but she didn't like the assumption that she and Dan were a married couple. She liked the way she was treated as a man better, getting to order her own food, not being ignored by the waiter like when she wore a dress. Liza spent most evenings with the librarian, so Lum would enter the Shays' home as the Adams Street Rooming House cook and exit as Mr. Columbus, who appreciated fine food and a brandy after dinner. But tonight she'd be going amongst Stoneham County people. Would anyone recognize her? Since Al and Margaret had already taken Caleb to the fair, they probably wouldn't be going back. Margaret had fussed about those poor freaks, saying it broke her heart to see them like that, like animals in the zoo. Lum had explained that they were making a living by traveling with the fair and that their families must not have wanted them.

Cyrus Snell had survived and, knowing that Smiley had saved his life, sent him to a doctor and bought him an artificial leg. The "condemned" sign was still on Al's and Margaret's land, and the government had tried to make them move in February, but Al had gone to the judge, who had issued an injunction until June, when the case would be heard. Margaret still complained about all the noise and dirt caused by the road development, because the injunction didn't stop the road running by Al and Margaret's land.

Walter was living in the porch room because Jimmy had sold the farm. Even though Jimmy had promised to include Lum in the decision, since only Walter and Jimmy's names were on the deed, they had taken a large settlement and given some to her. She had reminded them that the belongings were hers, and Dan had bought much of the furniture for the lodge and rooming house. Smiley was selling some of the things for her. Walter didn't want to sell, but was happy to have the money. He was helping Al, just as he had worked with his brother. Jimmy and Ethel were trying to sell their hogs so they could move to the new factory town. They most likely wouldn't be at the fair either.

After she had changed clothes, she noticed that Dan had on a new navy blue suit. "Mr. Columbus, next time we're in Roanoke, let's go to a tailor and get you a new suit."

"Oh, no. Won't he measure me?"

"That's what they do." Dan waved a magazine. "You should look in here and see a style you like. We can have them make one just for you." He handed her an *Esquire*, the cover showing a young man in front of a heavy desk, legs crossed at the ankle. A pleat sharp as a hen's beak went from waist to cuff. She enjoyed looking at all the young men with their fashionable clothes, but the idea of a tailor measuring her chest was out of the question. Did Dan think she really was a man when the suit was on? But tonight she'd get to see the Half-Man/Half-Woman with the other men. Would it be the same person who was on her postcard? She hadn't looked at it again but left it face-down at the bottom of her valise. As much as she looked forward to seeing Manfred/Matilda, she worried who else would be there, like the road workers who said she cooked like their mama or grandma. But they probably couldn't see her as anything other than the motherly figure that represented homemade food in a strange town.

Lum gained confidence the nearer to the fair she got. She liked striding beside Dan. Even though she liked wide skirts, they never allowed her to take the steps she wanted. The smell of animal dung, human sweat, and hay assaulted her nostrils when she entered the fairground, a wide space of hard-packed dirt off the highway where large road-building machinery often turned around. They passed the tents with the county's best livestock, and another tent for handmade pickles, canned goods, samplers, and quilts. A large banner had pictures of the Lost Aztec Children, Lobster Boy, Fat Lady, and Legless Woman, who was held by the Tallest Man. As soon as Lum and Dan paid to get into the ten-in-one tent, a huckster's voice rang out, "See the wild Seminole Indian from the swamps of Florida wrestle an alligator who's mad enough to tear him in two. He'll taunt him, he'll circle him, he'll jump on him. And you should see what the 'gator will do. New fight starts in ten minutes!"

"You want to see the alligator wrestler?" Dan asked.

"I already seen him, but you go on if you want." She remembered the Indian with his snaggletooth and tangled hair riding the alligator's back.

"Will you be all right?"

"Nobody will bother an old stiff like me." They both laughed at their recurring joke.

"Let's meet by the exit."

At each exhibit, she bought two cards from the act and had them signed. The Aztec Children smiled and giggled while a khaki-clad man with a pith helmet explained how they had been found in the Guatemalan jungle, the last of their tribe of Aztecs who had lived deep in the rain forests for centuries. The pointy-headed Aztecs seemed like children she'd known who were called "slow." Like the Melungeons, they had dark skin with straight black hair styled in what people called a bowl cut. The Lobster Boy sneered at the audience and was so rude when people asked questions that the crowd quickly moved on to the tiny Legless Woman in the arms of her giant husband. They seemed to truly be in love. Lots of questions were asked, but not the one on everyone's mind: How did they "do it"?

On one banner was an idealized, baby-like fat lady with dimpled cheeks and curly hair in a checkered dress with bows, but the real Fat Lady, Happy Hattie, wearing a bulky brown dress, reminded Lum of a stack of feed sacks. Her massive legs stuck out from beneath the skirt. When Lum stepped forward to buy two cards and get them signed, she asked Hattie if she knew the Siamese Twins, Daisy and Violet.

"Oh, what sweet girls. Well, at least Daisy was. That Violet, she'd say what was on her mind, let me tell you. When I was half my size, I was in a show with them for a short while. It was hard to get to know them because their owner kept them hidden when they weren't on display in the sideshow. So one time, all us sideshow people put on "Daisy and Violet Day." After the fair closed, we kept the midway open and the girls got to go on all the rides they wanted. Soon after, they left and started doing vaudeville shows. Never saw 'em again."

Someone asked Happy Hattie what she ate for breakfast, so Lum gathered her cards and exited, facing the smaller tent. A sign read: "Men only. No ladies or children allowed." One of the workers was waving men into the tent, calling out, "A little extra, just a nickel, to see something you've never seen before. Only for the strong of stomach, with a stout constitution. Come on in, sir, it's worth the pittance." The barker spoke directly to Lum, and she dropped a nickel into his palm and followed the man ahead of her into the tent. Her heart was pumping faster than a man running from a bear. The only light was a small lantern hanging from the center pole. Men shuffled around on the loose hay. A showman on stage kept saying, "Please wait, Manfred/Matilda is shaving and putting on lipstick." Or, "pulling up stockings and looking for a fedora."

Customers started to grumble to their neighbors, the word "morphydite" was repeated a few times, and the disgruntled voices rose. Light reflected off a silvery flask as it was raised to someone's mouth. Lum's heart pounded as if the bear were getting closer and she needed a tree to climb. Was it a mistake to come? Her father's voice came through, "Don't run. Don't play dead. Don't climb a tree. Don't look at the bear. Just back away." As much as she wanted to run, she didn't. She stayed.

Finally, someone appeared on stage—a grotesque combination of coiffed hair on one side, head shaved like a military recruit on the other. A tight undershirt revealed a flat chest next to a small but unmistakable breast as Manfred/Matilda turned one profile with lipstick to the audience, then the other, showing a mustache. The crowd stamped, yelling, "Take off your clothes," and "We paid to see your body." A chant went up: "Let us see, let us see, let us see!"

How dare they demand this person to strip? Lum thought, but she had to admit that she, too, was curious. *Is she—or is it a he—real? Will I ever see anyone who looks like me? Is there another anywhere in the world? The doctor, all those years ago, said he'd seen "one" in a book.*

The showman held up his hands. "Gentlemen, you will get your money's worth. Manfred/Matilda will show you what's what." Manfred/Matilda pulled off the blouse. Lum felt heat rise up her neck. She was embarrassed for Manfred/Matilda even if he/she wasn't. She looked at the stage and saw a nicely formed breast on one side and just a nipple on the other side of the chest.

Manfred/Matilda walked around, showing each profile. *But I'm not like that, my breasts are so large and there are two of them,* Lum thought. On stage, the skirt that had one pant leg was pulled down, the shoes were kicked off, and the undergarments came off, but the dim light didn't show much.

"How we know it ain't some woman?"

"Shine the light." The chant started up again, "Let us see, let us see!"

The person on stage stepped into the light at the front of the stage, penis in hand. Lum's knees buckled, remembering when her brothers pulled her dress up for a look. Manfred's thing was not like her own small part that Walter had called a wiener all those years ago. She wanted to cover Manfred/Matilda up. She'd been curious, but now wanted the show to end. She looked down, cheeks burning.

As the penis was stroked, the audience drew back. Feet shuffled, and men seemed to step farther away from their neighbors.

"Stop!" a voice called from the back. "That's not decent."

Was that the minister, or someone else who felt like the guardian of morals? The figure on stage stepped back.

Lum felt sullied. Bright lights blazed into her eyes when the tent flap flew open.

"Move on out, you've had your show," the announcer said.

Lum walked along the highway near Smiley's, chuckling to herself, thinking how the tables were turned. She couldn't wait to see the look on Smiley's face. He was back home, selling out of his house. Since he couldn't stand on his new leg for long, he didn't go around buying things, just waited for people to bring him items. More people were leaving for the new factory town, so they sold Smiley whatever they didn't want to take with them.

Approaching his house, she noticed him sitting in his wheelchair.

He waved, stood up, and started toward her but stopped at the edge of a table.

"Good morning. Got some cards for you," she called out.

"I knew you'd get me some," he said. "I'll bet they're signed and everything."

"Sure are." She stretched out her large hand, cards between the fingers. "Some of those folks don't look nothing like the banners."

"Don't matter. Folks won't know the difference. I sure appreciate you getting these for me. Every time I try to go to the fair, they say it's not Coloreds Night. Never will tell me when Coloreds Night is." Smiley flipped through the cards. "I just bought a box of junk from a couple of men who emptied out their daddy's top drawer. You want to look through it with me? Might be something you like. We can trade, or if you don't see nothing you like, I'll pay you." As he spoke, three flatbed trucks filled with tree trunks rumbled down the highway.

"How about giving me store credit?"

"Will do. You might want to spend it here in a minute. Let's take a look." He sat in his wheelchair and Lum sat next to him in her family's old graying dining room chair. He dug into the box and pulled out travel cards: Luray Caverns, waterfalls, hand-painted linen illustrations of grand hotels and railway stations, Western canyons, and cactus. After looking at each one, he handed it to her. He pulled out a "Eugene Debs for President" button and a flyer saying "No Conscription" with a picture of a bare-chested man. "I don't know what that means, but this man from the college likes things like this."

He paused, groaning. "Oh, no."

"What is it?" She looked over his shoulder at a picture of a blackened man on a burning pyre, his hands tied behind his back, and a large gathering of well-dressed men behind him. Scrawled on the other side read, "Enjoying a good ol' Bar-B-Q. Ha, ha. Go see *Birth of a Nation*. That'll straighten out your college thinking. As always, Junior." Dated August 12, 1907.

"Oh, how hateful!" Lum almost doubled over remembering the lynched man she'd seen. Did crowds gather everywhere as if a burning man, a hanging man, were a spectacle to be enjoyed? Had lynching really ended?

Smiley threw the postcard back in the box. "I'm sorry. I didn't know that was in there. I just got this box."

"Oh, Smiley. I'm sorry. Sorry you had to see that. I saw . . ." She didn't want to tell him. He'd think she was awful. Had he seen Clyde Jackson, too? Did he know him or his family?

Not knowing what to say, she turned toward the mountain. Sun shone through the fully-leafed walnuts, oaks, hackberries, and dogwoods, revealing a scar running alongside High Ford Road. She looked at the bare knob up top. Were the Melungeons still there? If not, where would they go? Was Kenny with his daddy and brother again? Did he dream of the Knob? Or her?

As she and Smiley watched the bulldozer working, a giant hemlock toppled to the ground with a loud thud. If she'd been closer, she would've felt the earth shudder.

Afterword

Intersex

Like many others, I originally knew about "hermaphrodites," and thought that they had organs of both genders. Intersex is the more accepted term for "a variety of conditions where a person is born with reproductive or sexual anatomy that doesn't fit the typical definition of female or male" (Intersex Society of North America). I imagine Lum as having congenital adrenal hyperplasia (CAH). Some of the books used in my research include: Katrina Karkazis, *Fixing Sex: Intersex, Medical Authority, and Lived Experience*, Durham, NC: Duke University Press, 2008; Alice Domurat Dreger, *Hermaphrodites and the Medical Invention of Sex*, Cambridge, MA: Harvard University Press, 2007; and Catherine Harper, *Intersex*, Oxford, UK: Berg, 2007.

Melungeons

I first heard about Melungeons through *The Devil's Dream,* by Lee Smith. Melungeons are isolated groups of people with dark skin and usually straight hair who lived in mountain communities in different parts of the South. Originally they were described as tri-racial, being the product of escaped slaves, American Indians, and whites. However, their origin has not been definitely established, with theories ranging from shipwrecked Portuguese sailors to Turkish or Moorish immigrants. Some of the books I used in my research include: N. Brent Kennedy with Robyn Vaughan Kennedy, *The Melungeons: The*

Resurrection of a Proud People; An Untold Story of Ethnic Cleansing in America, Macon, GA: Mercer University Press, 2001; Bonnie Ball, *Melungeons: Their Origin and Kin,* Johnson City, TN: Overmountain Press, 1992; Jean Patterson Bible, *Melungeons Yesterday and Today,* Rogersville, TN: East Tennessee Printing Company, 1975; and Wayne Winkler, *Walking Toward the Sunset: The Melungeons of Appalachia,* Macon, GA: Mercer University Press, 2005. For more books, see Mercer University's series on Melungeons.

Acknowledgments

First, I thank my mother, Fran Syfrett, for telling me stories of her childhood, including one about a "morphydite" who had no home of her own. And thanks to Karen Ladd for challenging me to write about her.

Being in a community of writers has been important. I'd like to thank Carol Lee Lorenzo for her helpful editing and suggestions. Members of my writing group—Charlene Ball, Linda Bell, Valerie Fennell, and Brenda Lloyd—as well as the revolving members of the Callanwolde and Fiction Intensives Workshops, have offered invaluable help in the many revisions of my book.

Special thanks to Elizabeth Knowlton and Linda Bell for closely reading the entire manuscript, not only with an eye to content, but also for excellent copyediting.

Much appreciation to The Hambidge Center for Creative Arts and Sciences, where a lot of writing and revising was done. Not only am I given the space and solitude to dedicate to my writing, but the setting in the Blue Ridge Mountains feeds my creativity.

To Brooke Warner, thanks for believing in *Lum*, to Cait Levin, who shepherded the book through multiple stages, and to Krissa Lagos, the eagle-eyed proofreader, and the whole She Writes Community, I couldn't have published my book without all your help. And thanks to Caitlin Hamilton Summie for all your assistance in getting my book out there.

Finally, I'd like to offer gratitude and love to my partner and fellow writer, Charlene Ball, for being my primary supporter and cheerleader. All through my writing of *Lum*, both as a member of my writing group and in other settings, she's offered suggestions and revisions, and has read different versions of the book in its entirety. We've spent many hours discussing our characters as if they were real people and having writing dates.

About the Author

© Charlene Ball

Libby Ware lived the first four years of her life in West Virginia and grew up in South Florida. She spent some childhood summers in the Blue Ridge Mountains of West Virginia and has always felt at home in the Appalachian Mountains. She is the owner of Toadlily Books, an antiquarian book business, and is also a book collector. She is a member of Georgia Antiquarian Booksellers Association, the Atlanta Writers Club, and the Georgia Writers Association, and she belongs to two writing groups. She is a fellow of The Hambidge Center for Creative Arts and Sciences. She was a finalist in the *Poets & Writers* Award for Georgia Writers, judged by Jennifer Egan, for a short story, "The Circuit," which is now Chapters 1–3 of this novel. She lives in Atlanta with her two dogs, Tilly and Robin, and a mile away from her partner, Charlene Ball.

SELECTED TITLES FROM SHE WRITES PRESS

She Writes Press is an independent publishing company
founded to serve women writers everywhere.
Visit us at www.shewritespress.com.

Hysterical: Anna Freud's Story by Rebecca Coffey
$18.95, 978-1-938314-42-1
An irreverent, fictionalized exploration of the seemingly contradictory
life of Anna Freud—told from her point of view.

The Rooms Are Filled by Jessica Null Vealitzek
$16.95, 978-1-938314-58-2
The coming-of-age story of two outcasts—a nine-year-old boy who
just lost his father, and a closeted young woman—brought together by
circumstance.

The Vintner's Daughter by Kristen Harnisch
$16.95, 978-163152-929-0
Set against the sweeping canvas of French and California vineyard life
in the late 1890s, this is the compelling tale of one woman's struggle to
reclaim her family's Loire Valley vineyard—and her life.

Bittersweet Manor by Tory McCagg
$16.95, 978-1-938314-56-8
A chronicle of three generations of love, manipulation, entitlement, and
disappointed expectations in an upper-middle class New England family.

Even in Darkness by Barbara Stark-Nemon
$16.95, 978-1-63152-956-6
From privileged young German-Jewish woman to concentration camp
refugee, Kläre Kohler navigates the horrors of war and—through
unlikely sources—finds the strength, hope, and love she needs to survive.

Pieces by Maria Kostaki
$16.95, 978-1-63152-966-5
After five years of living with her grandparents in Cold War-era
Moscow, Sasha finds herself suddenly living in Athens, Greece—caught
between her psychologically abusive mother and violent stepfather.

The Belief in Angels by J. Dylan Yates
$16.95, 978-1-938314-64-3
From the Majdonek death camp to a volatile hippie household on the
East Coast, this narrative of tragedy, survival, and hope spans more
than fifty years, from the 1920s to the 1970s.